Every Move

Every Move

Peter McPhee

James Lorimer & Company Ltd., Publishers
Toronto

First publication in the United States, 2004

James Lorimer & Company Ltd. acknowledges the support of the Ontario Arts Council. We acknowledge the support of the Government of Canada through the Book Publishing Industry Development Program (BPIDP) for our publishing activities. We acknowledge the support of the Canada Council for the Arts for our publishing program. We acknowledge the support of the Government of Ontario through the Ontario Media Development Corporation's Ontario Book Initiative.

The Canada Council | Le Conseil des Arts
for the Arts | du Canada

ONTARIO ARTS COUNCIL
CONSEIL DES ARTS DE L'ONTARIO

Cover design: Clarke MacDonald

Canada Cataloguing in Publication Data

McPhee, Peter, 1957–
    Every move / Peter McPhee

(SideStreets)
ISBN 1-55028-851-2 (bound).—ISBN 1-55028-850-4 (pbk.)

1. Harassment—Juvenile fiction. I. Title. II. Series.

PS8575.P44E94 2004   jC813'.54   C2004-904307-2

James Lorimer
& Company Ltd.,
Publishers
35 Britain Street
Toronto, Ontario
M5A 1R7
www.lorimer.ca

Distributed in the United States by:
Orca Book Publishers,
P.O. Box 468
Custer, WA USA
98240-0468

Printed and bound in Canada

*Special thanks to
Detective Gord Robertson
and Typewriter's mom,
Detective Beth Lowe,
both of the
Calgary Police Service.*

Chapter 1

Look at her. So beautiful, so perfect!

It had been a long wait, but it was worth it to surprise her. It was Tuesday, and gym was her last class of the day. She's wearing hardly any makeup and her red hair still looks slightly damp from the shower. Look at the way the wind ruffles it gently, how the sun plays on it.

How many times have I told her how much prettier she looks with just a touch of makeup? That she could get by without wearing any? Have I told her lately how perfect she is to me?

I can see through the lens that she's wearing a little eyeliner and it makes her blue-green eyes sparkle. I took the first couple of shots as she stopped at the top of the steps to talk to a blonde girl. I don't recognize the other girl. It's a warm afternoon for October, and she is wearing a light Adidas jacket over a plain white T-shirt. It's hard to believe that she will turn seventeen soon. I knew from the moment I first laid eyes on her that we were meant to be together.

And she knew it too.

I moved slightly to the left as she walked down the steps. She stopped when someone called her name, and I looked up to see Morgan running to catch up. Late as always.

I snapped two or three more shots as the two girls started to walk away from the school property. It's so easy to keep the focus on Emily. She stands at least three inches taller than her friend, and has this inner glow that would set her apart anywhere. It's not that Morgan isn't pretty in a tough kind of way; it's that Emily is so much more than just pretty. She could easily be the next supermodel. And I have the pictures to prove it. I've told her that a million times, she's just too shy to admit it to herself.

Morgan lets herself be chased by guys, and she tries to make Emily behave more like her. Emily ignores her. She's saving herself for the right guy, the only guy. Morgan still kids her about never having a boyfriend. I just laugh at that.

After all, what am I?

Chapter 2

Emily wiped the table with a practised swipe of her towel as she balanced empty mugs on her tray. The Cyber Taste Café was nearly empty, except for a group of obnoxious teenage boys huddled around a computer, shouting and swearing continuously. They had been there before her shift started twenty minutes ago and none of them had ordered anything. Their bill from the last server still sat on the table.

The only other customer was a regular. He sat at the back as well, in the opposite corner from the boys. He was a skinny, painfully shy boy who rarely looked up from the screen and never said a word except to order. Morgan, with her usual charm and compassion for others, had nicknamed him "The Geek-Freak." She had nicknames for all the regulars at the Cyber Taste Café, most of them obscene.

As Emily walked back to the counter she saw Ethan putting on his jacket.

"Where do you think you're going?" she shouted at him as he lifted the hinged top of the counter that separated the refrigerated display case from the cash area.

"Just out to the car," he answered, looking guilty at being caught sneaking out. "I left some supplies in the trunk."

"So why are you carrying a coffee?"

He shrugged. "Okay. Maybe I'll have a quick smoke as well."

"It better be quick. I'm on my own here."

"Won't be long, my dear. Promise," he said as he started to walk down the hall that led to the washrooms and the back door. The door led to the back alley, where a small picnic table sat next to the parking stalls. Employees took their breaks there when the weather was nice — to get fresh air and to cut themselves off from the customers. The Cyber Taste Café was on Ninth Avenue, a long stretch of restaurants, theatres, antique shops, upscale cafés, and patio bars. The avenue was the centre point of Inglewood, one of the trendy parts of Calgary that was a popular hang-out spot for all types of people.

"Besides, Morgan is never more than half an hour late."

"She called in sick, remember?"

"Right," he said. "You can handle it. I have the utmost confidence in you."

"Oh, yeah? Then what about a raise?"

Ethan kept walking, cupping a hand over his ear and shaking his head like he couldn't hear her. He disappeared down the hall that led to the back door. Emily sighed and looked at the clock, seeing she still had three more hours left. It was a bad sign when you counted the hours this early in the shift. Morgan wasn't really sick: she had a date, and Emily was covering for her, yet again. She had been Emily's best friend forever, had convinced her to take the job at the café so they could hang out together, but she was a terrible employee.

It was a good thing that Morgan and Ethan were so much alike.

Ethan was in his mid-thirties (at least that was Emily's and Morgan's guess). It was hard to tell. He wore his straight black (dyed) hair in a ponytail over his left shoulder, held in place by a series of ornate hair clip he changed daily to match his collection of eyeglasses. This evening he wore the silver glasses to match the silver Celtic pattern of his hair clip. Emily had been working at the Café for over six months and had yet to figure out her boss. Mostly he seemed to be walking through life in a self-involved daze. What he did best was amusing the customers while acting like he was still twenty years old. For the most part, he let Emily and the other girls who worked there take care of the day-to-day care and maintenance of the place. That was a good thing, since attention to detail wasn't really his strong point. Emily slipped behind the counter to lay her tray beside the sinks mounted on the west wall of the café. As she cleared the tray, the boys in the back started screaming and yelling, swearing loudly. She guessed they were playing some game on-line.

"Hey guys! Could you watch the language?" Emily shouted. She was hardly a prude, but it was annoying in a public place.

"What's your problem?" one of the boys replied. He was maybe a year younger than her, with bad acne and streaked hair. "There's no one in the joint!"

Just to bug her, they swore again, almost in unison. The kid with acne called her a few choice names. Emily debated going back to ask them to leave.

"Don't call her that," she heard someone say.

It was the regular customer, and it was the first time she had heard him speak without being spoken to first.

"Oh? Are we offending you, missy?" one of the other boys shouted back at him. The Geek-Freak just turned away, ignoring them. Emily watched as they glared at him for a while before going back to their game. She put away the mugs, wiping her hands on the green apron they all wore at work. As she poured her first coffee of the night, the noise started up again in the back. A couple of the boys had walked over to where the other boy sat by himself. They leaned over him, grabbing at the stuff he kept in a heavy backpack beside the computer.

Emily put down her coffee and started to walk to the back of the café. She felt her heart pound — nerves, she thought, and a little bit of irritation. She hated bullies. Emily had no idea what she would do once she got to them, but she had to do something.

The skinny boy in the corner wore his usual outfit, consisting of a faded army jacket, plaid shirt and worn cord pants. His dirty-blonde hair looked oily and messy, as if it had never seen a comb. He wore thick-framed glasses that he constantly pushed back onto the bridge of his nose. He was frantically trying to keep his things from the boys, who were grabbing them from the worn canvas backpack he kept them in.

"What's on these?" the acne-scarred boy asked, after freeing a small CD case. "Your porn-collection?"

"Load them up!" another boy shouted. "Let's all have a look."

The skinny boy ignored them and snatched the holder back with surprising quickness. He still kept his head down, not making eye contact with the others.

"Hey!" the boy yelled. "I want to see that." He started to reach for it again, but with that same quickness, the skinny boy pushed the holder into one of the deep pockets of his jacket, stood up suddenly, and, grabbing his knapsack, started to walk away from his tormentors.

The boys blocked his way, and Emily knew it was going to get worse. She walked between them.

"Alright, that's enough. I want you to leave!"

She regretted opening her mouth the minute the words came out. The lead boy spoke first, looking her up and down.

"Why the hell should we listen to you?"

"Because I work here." Even to her, it sounded pretty lame. She slid her hands into the pocket of her apron so the boys wouldn't see they were shaking. She glanced over her shoulder quickly. No sign of Ethan. The boys were enjoying every moment.

"He's the one you should kick out," one of the other boys said. "We caught him loading porn onto a disk. And we all know that that's against the rules here, right guys?"

The boys all shouted their agreement, following his lead.

"I saw what was going on," Emily replied. "Now I told you, I want you boys to leave. Now!"

"Who you calling boys, bitch?" another of them piped up, finding his courage.

Emily felt the last of her courage fade. She was alone right now and outnumbered. She had already dismissed the skinny boy as being useless if things got worse. Her shaking hands fumbled around nervously in her apron pockets and she felt something. It was a small plastic square. It took her a second to remember what it was — the indicator light from a coffee brewer that had snapped off on her last shift. She had put it in her apron to remember to have the brewer fixed, and then forgotten all about it. Inspiration struck, and she pulled the square out, holding it up for them to see.

"This is an alarm," she lied. "It's connected directly to the police. It takes them less than five minutes to get here. I pushed it …" she looked at the large railway clock on the wall for effect. "Oh, about a minute and a half ago."

"That's bull!" said the acne-scarred boy.

"Why don't you stick around and find out?"

"She's lying," the other brave one said.

"You really think my boss would let me work here at night without protection?"

This made them think. The acne-scarred leader shrugged.

"Come on guys, let's go." Still trying to look tough, they walked slowly but deliberately to the doors. The leader took a last swipe at the table, knocking the mugs and dishes to the floor. Emily just winced at the crash, but was relieved when she heard the bell over the door ring as the boys left, and knew the incident was over. Then she heard a terrible thumping noise, followed by screaming. Emily jumped back startled, and looked to see that the boys were screaming and pounding on the windows before they ran off down the street.

The skinny kid slipped past without even looking at her.

"You're welcome," she said to him, hoping he'd get the sarcasm in her voice. Next she looked at the mess on the floor. The mugs and dishes were made of heavy ceramic and only a couple of them were damaged. The worst part was all the spilled coffee and drinks. Emily turned away, heading back to the storage room to get a mop, and almost bumped into the skinny kid who had been standing behind her.

"Would you like some help?" he asked in a voice she could barely hear.

"It's okay. I can handle it," she replied, walking past him.

When Emily came back out, he was still standing there, head down, clutching the strap of his backpack and twisting it in his thin, pale hands. She nodded at him before kneeling down to separate the good mugs from the broken bits.

"That was a good bluff," he said. "Showing them that alarm thing."

Emily just nodded again and continued to clean.

"It's actually closer to four minutes."

"Pardon me?" she said, looking up at him.

He stood there, his eyes focussed on a point over her shoulder. She saw tiny round scars on the back of his pale hands, thick blue veins, and white knuckles.

"For the police to respond," he continued.

"Four minutes, three-point-seven-oh seconds, to be exact."

"Oh right. Well, I just wanted to get rid of those boys. And it worked, right?"

"Four minutes isn't fast enough. They could have hurt you. Remember the girl who was killed at the sandwich place last year? The police were two blocks away and responded in less than two minutes. It was still not fast enough."

"Okay! I get the point," Emily said. It came out a little harsh and she saw him nervously adjust his glasses.

"I don't really want to think about stuff like that, okay?" She stood as she spoke, dropping the broken pieces into a small trash bag on the wheeled mop bucket. He only nodded and looked at her, not saying a word. Emily placed the good dishes on the long counter that ran along the windows. She grabbed the mop out of the wheeled stand.

"I guess I have too much stuff in my head," he said. "I'm always on the Internet, looking up stuff. Like an information junkie." He grinned at that, as if it were a joke.

Emily said nothing.

"It's not porn on my discs. It's my backups and repair discs."

Emily just nodded and started to mop.

"I think porn degrades women."

She nodded again. She didn't feel like responding to that.

"I sometimes fix the computers I use here. They're messed up a lot. That's what I do. I fix computers."

"That's nice." Emily said as she mopped the floor, hoping he would just go. She was starting to think she liked him better when he never spoke. Maybe Morgan had picked the right name for him. He still stood there and she felt it was only polite to respond to him.

"Are you in a computer school?"

He smiled at that, with an odd, tight smile.

"We go to the same school. I'm a year ahead of you."

She looked up from her mopping, trying to place him. She couldn't recall ever seeing him in school.

"Sorry," she said. "I guess I haven't seen you around. It is a big school."

He nodded, not losing that odd smile.

"They're always looking for someone to fix them. You should talk to the owner."

"Could you?"

She saw that he seemed excited by the prospect. Emily immediately felt a bit guilty. She had only been making conversation, not dreaming that he would actually like the idea.

"Well, you might want to think about it. It's mostly nights …"

"That's okay. I like working nights."

Emily nodded, realizing she had stuck her foot in it this time. If he actually did get a job here,

Morgan would never let her live it down.

It was true that she tried to be nice to people — and that it had backfired on her more than once. The problem was that this time, she hadn't even meant to get involved.

"Well," she said at last. "I guess I could talk to Ethan."

"Did someone mention my name?" she heard his voice and turned around to see Ethan walking back into the café, smiling as he joined them. He actually enjoyed interacting with the customers. The smile slipped a bit as he saw Emily was mopping up.

"What's the mess?"

"Don't worry, boss," she said, hoping the sarcasm came through. "It's all under control." She decided to wait until later to tell him that the boys had also skipped without paying.

"So what are you two talking about, besides me?"

The boy looked at the floor, avoiding eye contact, twisting the strap of his backpack even tighter.

"Apparently he fixes computers," Emily said, nodding in the boy's direction. "And, even more amazing, he's willing to work for you."

"Really?" Ethan replied, looking happy, and reappraising the shabby boy standing next to him. "First. Are you dependable?"

Before he could answer, Ethan carried on.

"We've been looking for someone for ages. No

one lasts." He glanced back at the computer area, rubbing his hands gently together. "So. Where to begin?"

"How about seeing if he actually knows computers?" Emily suggested.

"Good idea," Ethan replied. "Let's go back and have a look, okay?"

They started to walk away, Ethan gently placing a hand on the boy's shoulder. Emily saw the boy move away slightly and Ethan lowered his hand. Ethan was a little too touchy for some people. She placed the mop back in the pail and started to walk away, pushing it along the tiled floor.

"My name's Ethan, by the way. And you are?"

"Michael," Emily heard him reply softly, "Michael LaVide."

Chapter 3

The day was still warm, so they sat at their favourite lunch spot, a bench under a huge oak tree in the park across the street from school. Calgary is a city obsessed with progress, anything old seems to get torn down. This park was still untouched and was filled with huge oaks, willows, and paper birches. It was just a short walk from there to the Bow River, and a weir that edged a bird sanctuary. Emily sat far away from the latest addition to the park this year, a yellow plastic box for junkies to deposit needles. Calgary's getting to be just another big city, she thought.

This was the first chance they'd had to talk all morning, and Morgan started immediately, filling Emily in on the gory details of her date last night. It wasn't so much a date as a chance to park somewhere secluded with a guy she hardly knew. Emily could have skipped the details.

As they were eating lunch, Emily let slip the events of the previous night at the café.

"You did what?" Morgan shouted. "You got the Geek-Freak hired?"

"I didn't get him hired," Emily replied. "Not exactly."

"I miss one shift," Morgan said dramatically, rolling her eyes toward the skies, "and you get into a fight *and* hire the biggest loser we know! Why couldn't you get some cute guy hired?"

"That's all we need. One more distraction for you at work."

Emily didn't point out that Morgan had missed a lot more than one shift.

"He said he goes to our school. Have you ever seen him?" Emily asked.

"No. But, if he goes to this school, he's getting beat up every day! I guarantee it."

Emily was sure of the guarantee. The chances were good that the very guys Morgan dated would be the ones giving the beatings.

Morgan shook her head. "He's actually going to work with us? That just creeps me out!"

"Oh, get over it! He's only going to be there when there's something wrong with the computers."

"Hello!" Morgan said. "That's only every day!"

Emily shook her head. It wasn't that bad. The guy was a nerd, but he was harmless.

"So, I told you the latest on my love life. What about yours?"

After a long sip of her water, Emily said, "When something happens, you'll be the first to know."

"Why are you waiting, Ems? Make something happen!"

"Just drop it, okay?" Emily said, shifting on the bench, a little uncomfortable about the direction of the conversation. Over the last couple of weeks, a certain guy had become a regular at the café, usually showing up with two or three of his friends to play around on the computers. Emily had begun to look forward to seeing him, and it seemed to her (reinforced loudly and often by Morgan and Ethan) that he was coming more and more to see her. All she really knew about him was his name, Daniel, and even that she had only picked up by listening to his friends.

Emily had a sudden, vivid memory. She was pouring coffee for Daniel, noticing his brown curly hair, green eyes, and white teeth grinning at her as he held out his cup. He said something that made her smile, words long forgotten. It didn't matter, the memory made her smile again.

"We both know I have a lousy track record with guys," Emily said.

Morgan turned to her friend. "Come on, Ems. Why can't you get over that?"

Emily didn't respond. She would be seventeen in March and had only had one boyfriend; in fact, she had had only ever dated one boy. It had ended so horribly. Justin had been sweet at the beginning, hiding the fact that he was insanely jealous and even abusive. Emily shook off the memory. She waited for Morgan to start her usual lecture about moving on. It didn't come this time.

"Oh — my — God!" Morgan said, staring off toward the school. "Is that who I think it is?"

Emily glanced at her, then looked to see what Morgan was talking about. A skinny boy with glasses, a faded army jacket, and a ratty backpack over his shoulder was waiting at the curb, looking for a break in traffic.

"Oh, God …" Morgan said, sitting up straight on the bench, watching as Michael LaVide started to cross the street, heading to the park.

"He isn't!" Morgan said as she drew her legs off the ground, bringing her knees up to her chest. "Oh, God. He is." she said, shaking her head and giggling as if disgusted. "He's coming right toward us. This is too gross."

Morgan punched Emily in the arm, hard. "This is your fault!"

Emily rubbed her arm and looked up at Michael as he stopped in front of her. Under the bright sun, he seemed paler than usual, and he was twisting the strap of his backpack so hard she saw red marks on his palm and fingers.

"Hi," Emily said at last, after nudging Morgan in the ribs — she now had her hands covering her mouth, trying to stop from giggling.

Michael nodded instead of answering. Emily waited a few beats. No response.

"Is there something we can do for you?" Emily asked. This seemed to set Morgan off, and she giggled uncontrollably.

"I just wanted to say hi," Michael said. "And, you know, to say thanks for getting me the job and all."

"I didn't exactly get you the job. But you're welcome."

Michael stood there silently again, staring at Emily, or maybe at a point just over her shoulder, it was hard to be sure.

"Is there something else?" Emily asked, wanting him to stop staring.

Michael reached into a side pocket of his army jacket. He pulled out a blue envelope and held it out to her, all without saying a word. Emily looked at Morgan and then at the envelope he held. She noticed that his hands were clean and the nails were cut so close to the quick they looked painful. She took the pale blue envelope.

"What's this?" she asked.

"It isn't much," Michael said. "It's just a thank-you note. I made the card myself."

He just stood there and Emily knew he was waiting for her to open it right at that moment.

"Well, thanks," she said. "I'll look at it later."

Michael's eyes shifted toward Morgan for an instant and then returned to the spot over Emily's shoulder.

"Okay," he said. "Nice talking to you again. Bye."

And with that he turned around and marched off. Morgan stopped giggling and laughed out loud as they watched him walk away, shifting the backpack on his narrow shoulders. Emily couldn't believe what had just happened.

"Open it!" Morgan said at last.

"That was so rude, Morgan," Emily said. "Even for you!"

She tried to sound harsh, but she knew she was smiling as well. Morgan had always had a contagious laugh.

"Oh, who cares? A geek like him has seen worse! Now open it!"

Emily hesitated, not ready to open it just yet. Morgan snatched it from her hand.

"Jesus, wimp! Let's have a look." She carelessly ripped the blue envelope open, tearing a corner of the card inside. Morgan pulled it out quickly. She looked at it and then tilted her head to the side, her lips forming a sarcastic pout.

"Aww! Isn't it precious?"

Emily tried to grab the card back from her friend's hands. "Lemme see!" she shouted.

Morgan stood up, keeping the card out of reach. "Wait. Let me read it to you."

She cleared her throat before reading out loud: "Dear Emily. Words cannot describe your kindness to me. I'm sure this is the beginning of a great friendship. Respectfully yours, Michael."

Emily shook her head. She didn't know what to say.

"Oh, and there's a PS," Morgan said. She began to read: "I often picture you naked when I'm in the shower."

"It does not say that!" Emily said, trying to grab the card again. Morgan lifted it high in the air and spun around, keeping it just out of reach.

"I wouldn't worry about it. I doubt he showers very often."

Emily made one last lunge and grabbed the card. She turned away to read it, Morgan still giggling and reading over Emily's shoulder. At first she thought the type was computer-generated, but then she saw that it was handwritten in a fluid, beautiful script. The writing style and the words seemed ornate, as if from a past century.

"Look at the picture on the front," said Morgan.

Emily flipped the card over. On the front was a photograph of her. In the picture she was looking away from the camera, her head tilted up and her long, auburn hair shining brightly in the sun. It was actually one of the best photographs she had ever seen of herself.

"Did you pose for that?" Morgan asked.

"And when would I have done that?" Emily replied.

"How did he get it, then?"

Emily shook her head.

"It's weird," Emily said. "But it is kind of …"

Before she could finish, Morgan pointed a warning finger at her. "Don't you even think of saying it!"

Emily laughed. "Come on. It is sweet! Look at all the trouble he went to."

"It isn't sweet. It's psycho."

Emily looked at the photograph again, admiring Michael's obvious talent once more. And it was amazing that he had worked so hard to get it done for today. She wondered when he had taken the photograph. Then she frowned, realizing which blouse she wore in the photo. It was one that could only be dry cleaned, one that she had given to her mother to take in with the next order.

It was a blouse she hadn't worn in almost two weeks.

Chapter 4

Emily slid behind the counter and opened the door to the storage room to get her apron. Morgan was sitting next to Ethan and both of them were looking at her oddly.

"What?" she asked. Morgan and Ethan said nothing, just shifted their eyes quickly to the right as if indicating something. She didn't know what they were trying to say, and then she felt her heart skip a beat. Was Daniel here already?

She quickly scanned the café and saw that only one of her tables was occupied at the moment. A couple sitting at the window ledge caught her eye. She smiled but didn't rush over to see if they were ready to order. They were regulars and lousy tippers. The only other customer was an older woman sitting at a computer near the back.

No Daniel, Emily saw. She had hoped that was what Morgan and Ethan were trying to hint at. She didn't really expect Daniel to be here so early, her shift only started at six. She wasn't even sure if he would come this evening, since he hadn't really made a firm commitment. It was more of a vague "maybe I'll see you on Tuesday" kind of thing. That had been on Sunday, her previous shift at the café. It would be perfect if he did show up tonight. Tuesday was usually the slowest night of the week, which meant they might even have a chance to talk.

"Wrong direction," Morgan said at last, still moving her eyes as if indicating something. Ethan was doing the same thing. Emily had no idea what they were up to. Then she saw a small gold-foil box sitting next to the cash register. Emily knew what it was and rolled her eyes, letting out a small groan of annoyance.

"Not again."

Just then, the bell over the door chimed, indicating more customers had arrived. Emily, still staring at the box, could tell they were headed to the north wall and Morgan's tables. Morgan grabbed her order book and patted Emily on the back as she slipped past her. "You should be flattered. Not everyone has a secret admirer."

"He's hardly secret if I see him every day!" Emily said. Morgan just shrugged as she walked to her section. Emily wrapped the strings of her green work apron around her waist, tying them at the back. After a moment of thought, she picked up the gift sitting on the counter.

Ethan said "Mmm! Bernard Callebaut! My favourite. Nothing like a good box of Belgian chocolates. You have to share!"

Emily just stared at the box in her hand. Ethan gave her a gentle push on her shoulder. "Oh, go on. Open it. It doesn't mean anything!"

She wasn't so sure. It was the third gift Michael had left. One for every week he had been working at the café. So far, she hadn't said a word about the unwanted gifts. She thought she was well on the way to giving him the wrong impression of the kind of relationship she wanted. He had made it pretty obvious what he wanted by the gifts and the notes attached to them.

Shortly after starting to work at the café, Michael LaVide had begun to e-mail her. Emily wondered how he had found her address, but guessed it wouldn't be much of a challenge for a computer geek. Just to be polite, she replied to the first few. His e-mails were all innocuous and boring, full of useless information that he thought would make him seem more interesting to her. He was wrong. After those first few, she didn't respond and hoped that it would stop. The e-mails had continued. And the gifts.

Morgan slipped back behind the counter, starting to fill her order.

"You still haven't opened it?" Morgan said, incredulous. Ethan shook his head.

"Come on. Let's see what he got you this time!"

"If it's a sampler, I call the orange cream!" Ethan cried out. He took the box began to pull off the small plastic seal along it edge.

"Don't open it! I don't want another gift from him!"

"Oh! Too late." Ethan exclaimed as he pulled the lid open. Morgan leaned over as she poured coffee from the urn. She was smiling, then wrinkled her nose in disgust.

"Ew! Gross! Not those!"

For a split-second, Emily didn't want to look inside the box, afraid that Michael had done something disgusting. But curiosity made her look into the box.

"What do you mean gross? It's orange peel, yum!" Emily told Morgan. "How many times have you seen me eat them?"

"They're still gross. They always look like worms."

"Worms?" Ethan asked. "Who would make chocolate-covered worms?"

"I don't know. It's made by some French guy, right?"

"Belgian," Ethan replied.

"Whatever," Morgan said.

Emily ignored the banter and took the gift card from the box. She turned it over and saw the ornate logo of the manufacturer, and underneath that, the now familiar script of Michael LaVide. It read:

"Enjoy. I know this is your favourite. Love,

Michael."

Emily frowned and looked away from the card, seeing Ethan take a few of the orange peels. He lifted them close to Morgan's mouth.

"Here, try them!"

"Get away!" Morgan laughed, lifting a hand to push them away.

"Come on, they're good!" Ethan said. "Look." He slipped a few into his mouth and smiled. "You have to let them melt in your mouth."

"No way are those things getting near my mouth." she was grinning as Ethan playfully tried again to make her eat one. Emily looked at the card again. The words on it bothered her: I know this is your favourite.

And then, even more disturbing: Love.

It was true that orange peels were her favourite, but … "How did he know I like these?" she said, perplexed.

"You must have mentioned it to him," Ethan replied. He had given up trying to force-feed Morgan.

"But when? I mean, I've barely spoken to the guy."

"He probably heard you tell someone," Morgan said. "He's always just sitting there all quiet, working away on the computers. He probably listens to everyone's conversation, the perv!"

"Come on," Ethan said. "Michael's a fellow employee. Don't call him names. He's just …" Ethan paused, trying to think of the right word to describe Michael. "Oh, I don't know … He's just different."

"Yeah, he's different all right!" Morgan said. She organized four coffee cups onto her tray and slipped past Ethan. He was still picking away at the chocolate.

"Well, whatever. He's good at keeping my computers running. And he's cheap."

"Maybe you should pay him more so he can afford to buy stuff. Like soap." Morgan added as she went back to her table.

"You are a terrible person. And such a cynic for one so young."

Emily was still thinking about the words on the card: "Love, Michael." It made her re-think some of the things he had said in his e-mails. He had told her many times about how he knew fate had drawn them together, that their friendship would last forever. She wondered now if he meant something more intimate than just friendship. She stood up, tossing the card on the counter beside the box of chocolates. She would have to set Michael straight. Once and for all.

Emily went over to the sink and began to wash her hands as the bell over the door chimed again. She looked back to see three guys walk in and head straight to the computer section.

It was Daniel and his friends.

He glanced over at her before stopping at a table by the window, and she thought he smiled at her. She smiled back at him and felt a little foolish seeing that he had already turned his back to her as he sat down. She glanced at the mirror over the sink, pushed a strand of her auburn hair back from her forehead, and grabbed a tray and her notepad before heading to the table. The best part was that neither Morgan nor Ethan had noticed Daniel yet.

"Your table," Morgan said.

Emily nodded and smoothed out her apron. Morgan finally took one of the orange peels out of the box and studied it. Emily snatched it from her and popped it in her mouth. Two of her favourite things were in the café right now.

Orange peels and Daniel.

All thoughts of Michael disappeared as she walked to the back as coolly as she could and watched as Daniel turned to smile at her. As she did, she heard Morgan shout.

"Hey, these worms aren't bad!"

Chapter 5

"Hi," she said as she walked up to the table. Daniel grinned at her, and she hoped she looked a whole lot calmer than she felt. Stupid, she thought. He's just some guy you serve coffee to. He probably hasn't had a second thought about you since Sunday. Emily was amazed at her feelings; it had been so long since she had been interested in a guy.

"Oh, hey," he replied casually, but with a wide smile.

The other two boys sat at a computer station right next to Daniel. They made a hooting sound and nudged each other gently, laughing. Emily felt herself blush, wondering what the joke was. Then she saw Daniel blush and knew that the joke was on him, not her. The boys got up from the computer and walked over to the table. One of the friends, a slightly overweight boy with thick blond hair, punched Daniel on the shoulder.

"Oh, hey?'" the blonde boy said, imitating Daniel. "That's all you're going to say to her?" The other boy, dark-haired and wearing an expensive skater jacket and shoes, looked over at Emily.

"All he's talked about since Sunday is coming here tonight. And now he acts all cool!"

"I did not! Just shut it, Al!" Daniel said, his cheeks flushing, annoyed by their teasing. He ran his hand through his dark, wavy hair and looked around the place, avoiding eye contact with her.

"Well, it is pretty good coffee here," she said. She immediately regretted saying anything.

"Oh, he's not here for the coffee," the blonde boy said. Daniel shook his head and then looked at her finally, smiling faintly as if to apologize for their behaviour.

"Okay," she said, her waitress persona taking over. It wasn't as if it this was the first time she'd had a bunch of boys acting like jerks in here. "We also have Chai drinks and milkshakes on special tonight."

"I'll have a coffee," Daniel said.

"We have several different blends …"

"Just the normal kind," he said rather sharply.

Emily noticed the tone and felt a little hurt, but the waitress persona was still in charge.

"And what would you like?" she asked, turning to the other two. They placed their orders and she wrote them down before she walked quickly away from the table. When she reached the counter,

Ethan and Morgan were waiting, grinning at her.

"So? How's the other boyfriend tonight?"

Emily ignored her as she went behind the counter to fill the orders.

"He doesn't look like he's in a good mood."

"I think his friends are embarrassing him," Ethan said.

Emily shrugged as she filled the first coffee mug. She was pretty annoyed. She had looked forward to this shift since Sunday, and now Daniel's stupid friends had spoiled it. Why did he have to bring them anyway? Once more the bell rang over the door and a group of people wandered in. They walked past the counter and straight to Morgan's section.

"I guess I better get to work," Morgan said as she stood.

Emily was glad for the distraction. Her order filled, she placed the drinks on the tray and walked back to Daniel's table. His two friends had gone to sit at the computer again, both of them looking intently at the monitor. Daniel now sat alone and he managed to smile at her as she placed the mugs on the table.

"Thanks," he said, lifting the mug. "Looks good."

She nodded and started to turn away, not ready to forgive him for acting like a jerk in front of his friends.

"Look," he said, and touched her arm gently. She turned to face him. "Sorry about that. The guys were acting stupid. But they were right, I was looking forward to coming here tonight."

"Because of the coffee?" She felt herself relax a bit.

"Yeah. And, you know. Because I wanted to talk to you."

She was facing him now, smiling. "About what?"

He grinned and shrugged. "I don't know. Nothing in particular. Just talk is all."

The bell rang and more people came in. Why does it have to start getting busy now, she thought?

"Well the conversation's been fascinating so far," she said. He laughed at her sarcasm. She remembered how much she liked his laugh. Tonight got off to a bad start was all, Emily told herself.

"It'll be brilliant, I promise," he said.

"We'll see. Right now I have to get to work."

"When do you get a break?"

Emily glanced at the clock over the door. "In about an hour."

He looked a little disappointed at that.

"It's usually slow on Tuesdays, so maybe I can talk a bit sooner."

"Great," he said, smiling.

Of course, the café stayed busy for the next three hours. It was a warm fall evening, drawing out both locals and tourists. The café itself was usually filled with a typical Calgary crowd, yuppies wearing two thousand dollar designer eyeglasses sitting at a table next to cowboys in Wranglers and Stetsons.

Sometime between their first round of coffee and the sudden rush, Daniel had joined his friends at the computer. Emily had refilled their mugs several times but never had the chance to say more than a few words to Daniel. It was almost ten when the crowd began to thin out again and she realized that the break she was supposed to have mid-way in her shift had never happened. As she was giving change to the last of her customers, she saw Daniel and his friends walking toward her, putting their jackets on. Daniel held the bill and handed it to her. Their fingers touched slightly as she took it from him.

"So," he said. "Busy night, huh?"

"Is that the brilliant conversation you promised me earlier?" she said, grinning.

He smiled back. "You want to talk about the weather?"

She rang in his bill. "That'll be $18.50," she said.

"Whoa! This place is expensive!" said the chubby blonde boy. She thought his name was Rick.

"Most of it was your extra large mocha's!" Al the skater kid said, patting Rick's belly. He quickly pushed Al's hand away. Al then turned to Daniel.

"Since it was you who wanted to come here so

40

much, buddy, why don't you leave the tip?"

The two boys handed Daniel some money and then headed for the door.

"We'll leave you two alone," Rick said, laughing.

Daniel just looked at her and rolled his eyes. He reached into his pocket and pulled out a pile of coins. "So what's a good tip on an eighteen dollar bill?"

"Don't worry about it," she said.

"No. I want to. Even though I think the service could have been better."

Emily crossed her arms. She was exhausted but wasn't going to let him get away with that.

"Oh, really? And what was wrong with the service?"

"Well, for one thing, the waitress wasn't very friendly."

"In case you didn't notice, the waitress was pretty busy."

"Yeah, but she did promise to talk to me later."

"Well. It's later now."

He grinned. "Too late. It is a school night."

"Oh well," Emily said, acting casual. "Maybe some other time."

He stepped a little closer to her, leaning over the counter slightly. She found herself leaning slightly toward him.

"Maybe I could call you?"

"You think I just give my number to any boy who comes in the place?"

"Well, I am a regular now."

She leaned back and wiped a strand of hair from her forehead.

"Tell you what. Do you have e-mail?" she said.

"Why wouldn't I?"

"Well, you do hang out at a cyber café a lot."

"That's because the coffee is so good."

She walked around the counter, brushing past him.

"Follow me," she said.

They walked to the rear of the café and she sat down at one of the computers. She connected to her e-mail server and logged into her personal account while he stood behind her.

"What's your address?" she said, ready to type.

"Here. Let me," he said, leaning over her to put his hands on the keyboard. She turned to look up at him and saw that their faces were only inches apart. For an instant, neither of them said a word, they just looked into each others eyes. His eyes were a dark green, almost the exact colour of hers.

"Are you going to type or not?" she said finally.

He typed in his e-mail address and she was about to hit the send button. Daniel put his hand over hers, stopping her.

"Wait," he said. "What's the subject heading?"

She looked at his hand and he hesitated before lifting it away. She clicked on the subject box and typed: FRIENDSHIP. Then she hit the send button.

"There. Now if you want, you can reply."

"Friendship?" he asked, smiling. "I hope my spam blocker doesn't get it first."

Then Emily looked away, standing up. Daniel stood up as well, looking a little awkward.

"Can I reply tonight?"

"How long does it take you to get home?" she said.

"Maybe an hour."

"I'll be up. In case you send me a message."

"Count on it."

He grinned and walked out. His buddies were waiting outside, and through the windows she saw them start to kid him as he joined them. Daniel waved at her as the three of them walked quickly away. She noticed that the place was now empty. Great timing, she thought.

As she walked behind the counter, she brushed past Morgan sitting on the stool by the cash and grinning.

Then she remembered something. She shook her head and laughed.

"What is it?" Morgan asked.

"He never gave me my tip."

"Oh, well. I say dump him right now."

They both laughed. And then Emily saw Morgan's expression change: a coolness came over her features as she saw something behind Emily. She turned to look.

Michael LaVide was walking out of the computer area. As usual, he wore the faded army jacket, the canvas backpack gripped tightly in his right hand. He stopped at the other side of the counter and just stared at her, not speaking or moving, except to push his glasses back on the bridge of his nose. It was as though he was waiting for her to say something.

"Hi, Michael," Emily said. "I didn't know you were here."

"Was that guy bothering you?"

Emily was a little startled by Michael's tone. He seemed upset about something. It was a little unsettling, since he never showed much emotion. This new mood was in complete contrast to the breathless, cliché-filled e-mails he sent her. She saw a little twitch over his right eye, and his tongue was flicking back and forth across his thin lips.

Emily had been startled at his sudden appearance, but then her approach changed to her normal one for Michael, speaking softly and carefully, the way one would speak to a child.

"No, Michael. He wasn't bothering me."

"Who is he?"

Now he was starting to annoy her.

"Just a friend."

He stepped closer to her. Emily instinctively stepped back, even though the counter was still between them.

"I thought he was just a customer."

"He's both." She didn't like the intense look in his eye.

"Is there something I can do for you, Michael?"

It was Ethan's voice.

Emily turned to see her boss, relieved to have an excuse to end the conversation. Michael's behaviour was unsettling. It wasn't so much what he asked, but more his body language, his obvious agitation. Michael ignored Ethan and continued to stare at Emily.

Ethan spoke again.

"Michael? What are you doing here tonight?"

"Emily and I were having a private conversation." His pale face was flushed and he seemed furious.

Ethan gave Emily a questioning look, as if to say "what's going on?" but she just shrugged. She raised her hands and shook her head, indicating to Ethan that she had no idea what was going on. And then Michael's anger seemed to vanish as soon as it had appeared, and the usual mild Michael stood there, once again staring off at some point in space.

"I'm sorry. Did I interrupt?" Ethan's tone was slightly sarcastic.

"It's okay," Michael said, missing Ethan's sarcasm. "We have plenty of time to talk later, right Emily?"

Emily just scowled. Michael continued to speak to Ethan without looking directly at him.

"I just came in because station four was acting up. Someone messed it up trying to crack the firewall. I can fix it no problem."

Ethan glanced over at Emily and they

exchanged a look, both of them realizing how oddly Michael was behaving.

"Okay," Ethan said. "But, I didn't ask you to come here tonight."

Emily noted a firmness in Ethan's voice she had never heard before. Gone was his usual casualness, the eager-to-please Ethan she knew.

"It's okay. Station four is messed up. I can fix it." Michael started walking down toward the computers.

"I don't think you get my point. I don't want you fixing computers unless I call you in."

Michael continued to stare straight ahead, as if he hadn't heard what Ethan had said. Emily felt a presence behind her and saw that Morgan had moved closer.

"Do you understand what I said, Michael?"

Finally the boy looked at him, just for a second. His whole face kind of twitched and he looked away again, this time he stared through the windows at the cars flashing past on Ninth Avenue.

"I can fix it easily."

"I know that." Ethan said in the same calm but stern voice. "I realize that it's been only a few weeks since you started, so I want you to understand that you can't show up anytime you want. Let me call you when something needs fixing, okay?"

He smiled as he said this, trying to keep the moment as light as possible. Michael continued to stare out the window.

"It's okay," he said at last to the room in general. "No charge. It makes my job easier is all."

Ethan nodded at that. "I see. Why don't you come back tomorrow morning to fix it?"

Ethan waited a few seconds for a reply, but Michael didn't speak, he just stood there, his jaw working.

"Why don't you go home, Michael?" Ethan said. It was an order, not a request. Finally Michael turned to Emily.

"There's a few things we have to discuss," he said to her. "Just the two of us."

"No, Michael," Emily replied. "Good night."

She turned her back to him and started to untie the loops of her apron. She took her time slipping it over her head and didn't turn back till she heard the chime ring over the door and knew he was gone. Morgan caught Emily's eye and raised her hands to her face, jaw dropping open.

"What was that all about?" she asked. Emily just shook her head. As she hung her apron up in the storage room, she saw her hands were trembling slightly. When she came back out, Ethan took her and Morgan by the arm.

"Come on ladies, let's clean up and close a little early tonight, shall we?"

Emily glanced at the big clock over the door. It was only five minutes to closing.

"You better not stiff us our full pay!" Morgan said, giving him a gentle shove.

"Would I do something like that?" Ethan

replied, pretending to be hurt. The three of them started to shut the place down, Morgan turning off the coffee urns and draining them. Emily opened the dishwasher, sliding out the trays to begin loading it. Ethan sat at the cash register to begin tallying the night's receipts.

"We still have to bring the sign in," he said, his hands full of cash.

Morgan swore and looked out at the sidewalk. Near the curb was the sandwich-board sign that had the café logo and a chalk area where they displayed the specials. It was heavy as lead. If you worked the early shift, you had to drag it out every morning, and the evening shift meant you had to drag it back inside.

"Wait a minute," Morgan said. "How did Michael know about the firewall thing?"

"What?" Ethan said in mid-count.

"I mean, how did he know to come in to fix it?"

Ethan shrugged as he tossed the receipts into a blue, zippered pouch.

"He's a computer geek. They know stuff like that."

"How? Is he psychic as well?" Morgan asked.

"He probably just came in to make sure Emily got the chocolates, and then he made up that lame excuse when he got caught," Ethan replied.

The question bothered Emily as she and Morgan stepped outside to get the sign. Neither of them had bothered to put on their jackets, and although it was a warm night for early November,

48

it was still chilly. Emily saw Morgan shiver.

"Let's get this over with fast," Morgan said, running to the side that faced the street. Emily was about to grab the sign when she heard a voice.

"Can I help?"

She stood up straight, startled. Michael stepped out from between parked cars and walked toward her. She instinctively backed away from him. Morgan stood and rushed around the sign to step between her and Michael.

"Why are you still here?" she shouted.

He ignored her and kept looking at Emily, still walking to her. Morgan shoved him hard in the chest. Michael staggered back, looking at his chest in surprise, then glaring at Morgan. Emily saw Morgan lean away from him, just as she had seen Ethan do earlier.

"What do you want Michael?" Emily asked to fill the sudden stillness.

"We need to talk. I told you that."

"We have nothing to talk about."

He smiled at her, the strange half-smile that made him look even creepier.

"Did you get the gift?"

"I did, Michael. But please stop giving me gifts. It's not necessary."

"Of course it's necessary. How else would you know how I feel?"

"Look, Michael," she said a bit more firmly. "No more presents, okay?"

He didn't speak for a moment. Then his look

became happy like he knew a secret.

"Okay. Just one more. And it's a great one. You'll see."

"I don't want any more candy. Or cards," she said.

"I know that!" he said, laughing suddenly. "It's a surprise. It'll be fun, you'll see."

"Michael, look," she said, raising her voice. "I don't want anything else from you. Understand?"

Emily hated being this harsh to anyone, but he just didn't seem to get normal signals from people. Michael shoved his hands deep in the pockets of his army surplus jacket and stepped back.

"I thought we were past all this, Ems. I know you still don't trust guys because of Justin."

Emily felt the colour drain from her face, felt a sudden rage. She tried hard to fight it. When she spoke, she could hear the anger in her voice.

"What do you know about that?"

"Come on. It's me you're talking to."

"How do you know about that?" she repeated. She was no longer aware of the chill in the air.

Michael shrugged. "I knew about it before we met. A lot of people heard. You know how it is in school."

Morgan stepped forward until her face was only inches from Michael's.

"Shut your damn mouth! You understand me, creep? Just shut up and turn around and walk away before I break your neck!"

Michael didn't look at her. He stared off at

some distant point over Emily's shoulder. After a second or two, he turned around and walked stiffly down the avenue. Morgan grabbed Emily, pulled open the café door and practically shoved her through. Inside, she slammed the door shut and locked it. She looked through the windows and saw that Michael was gone before turning back to Emily. Ethan had walked over to them, obviously wondering what had happened.

"If that creep had come back in, I'd have killed him!"

"Michael?" Ethan asked. "He was outside?"

"He was waiting for Emily."

For once, Ethan didn't try to make a joke. It was obvious that Michael had upset both girls terribly. Emily was still thinking about what he had said outside about Justin: "A lot of people heard. You know how it is in school." It had been almost two years, but the memory still hurt. She knew it was only her imagination, but sometimes she still felt the bruises Justin had left on her body.

Chapter 6

Half an hour later, after finally retrieving the out-door sign without another Michael sighting, Emily and Morgan left the café, walked across the railway tracks heading for their street in Ramsey, the neighbourhood adjoining Inglewood and the café.

The street they lived on was perched on top of a high sandstone cliff overlooking a wide ravine. Because of the sharp drop-off from the cliffs, most of the homes on the street were on the east side, facing the ravine and the city park that followed the edge of the cliffs. The park ended at the fences of the few houses that actually sat on the cliffs. Emily's house was dead centre between them. Morgan's house was directly across the street from hers. They had always been best friends, for as long either could remember, sharing their deepest secrets as well as their clothes. It had been a while since Emily had borrowed anything of Morgan's, since she was not wild about the retro-style her friend had adopted recently.

Beyond Emily's backyard was a deep valley that contained railway yards and the ever-increasing grounds of the Calgary Stampede. Framing them were the office towers of downtown. The Calgary Tower, which had been one of the largest buildings when she was growing up, was now dwarfed by skyscrapers, its revolving restaurant looking like a red cupcake perched on top of a narrow concrete pedestal.

That night there was a full moon and Emily could easily make out the city skyline, even the faint outline of the Rockies far to the west. Luminous clouds, lit by moonlight, scudded along their peaks.

There had always been a rhythm to her life on this street, closely following the seasons and the rhythms of the city. In the spring, on Victoria Day, there were always the fireworks on the Stampede ground. She and her parents would bundle up on their back porch under blankets with mugs of hot chocolate and watch the display. Their house had the best view of the fireworks in the city. It was part of the tradition for her friends to sleep over that night, and all of them would stay up to watch. Recently, her parents had remodeled their kitchen and added a sunroom that overlooked the ravine. It made it possible to watch the sun set behind the mountains no matter what the temperature was outside.

In the summer it was the Stampede, the sound and lights of the midway echoing across the valley until late into the night, reflecting back from the sandstone cliffs. She could hear the voice of the announcer blaring out the action of the chuck-wagon races. In winter there was tobogganing down the more gentle slopes of the hills, ice skating in the local rink. Her house had always been the central gathering place for her friends, a second home for most of them. All of her friends thought her parents were the coolest, and there were times when Emily thought so as well. Her house was a place where they had all felt safe to be themselves, a refuge from the outside world.

It would be hard to leave this place after next year, to go to university on the West Coast.

"I've said it like a million times," Morgan was saying, between sips of the hot mocha she had made to take out at the café. "I just don't get you."

"What is it now?" Emily asked, already knowing the answer.

"Hello? I mean, for like a month now you've had a crush on this Daniel guy, and when he asks for your number, you tell him to e-mail you."

"I still hardly know the guy. He's someone who comes in to the café. I don't even know what school he goes to or where he lives."

"So that's why you give him your number. So he can call you and you can talk about stuff like that." Morgan replied. "That's what the telephone was invented for. And, then, maybe you can actually see the guy, instead of having two minutes at a time at work. If it were me, we'd already be going out."

"Yeah, well, we both know I'm not you. I like to move slower. A lot slower."

"Are you implying I'm easy?" Morgan said, half-smiling.

"Who's implying?"

Morgan pushed Emily. "Well at least I'm not going for the title of world's oldest living virgin."

Emily just laughed at that. She had heard all the comments about her reluctance when it came to guys. Even before Justin, there was something that bothered her about the way boys hung around in packs, leering and whispering to each other. After what had happened between her and Justin back in the ninth grade she had little reason to trust boys. That was why it was surprising she was attracted to someone once again. They walked half a block or so before Morgan spoke again

"So what do you know about him?"

Well," Emily said. "I know he's our age. I know that he likes his coffee black with two sugars. And he's into blues music."

"That much, huh?" Morgan teased. "Well, if you don't make a move, I will. He's pretty cute. In a curly-haired, skinny, dorky kind of way."

"Oh come on! Even you wouldn't do that to your best friend. And he is not dorky!"

Morgan took another sip of her mocha, then

blew bubbles in it with a brown plastic straw. She said nothing.

"Tell you what," Emily said. "Next time he comes in, I'll introduce you to his friends."

"Oh, please! I wouldn't be caught dead with either of them. Especially the fat one. He is so gross!"

Emily just shook her head. "He's not fat. Just a little bit out of shape."

"Yeah, like Ethan's just a little bit gay!"

"Would you stop it?" Emily shouted, laughing at her friend's usual outrageous comments. "Ethan is not gay. He's just …"

"Just what?" Morgan asked interrupting Emily's thought.

"I don't know," Emily said, still laughing, trying to think of how to describe her boss. "Ethan is just … neat."

"Neat? Like how the hippies say neat? Like, is he groovy too?"

"No! I mean he's neat, well-dressed. And he always smells nice. That kind of neat."

"Oh, neat! Now I get it." Morgan was silent a moment, except for the sound of her sucking the mocha through her straw.

"Of course you do understand that when someone calls a guy neat, it really means gay, right?"

"You are so terrible! And such a homophobe!"

"Me? No way. In fact, some of my best friends are neat."

She slipped an arm over Emily's shoulder,

pulling her closer. "Take you, Ems. You are one neat girl."

Emily laughed and squirmed out of Morgan's grasp. "You are a lousy friend! Just because I don't give a guy my number I'm suddenly neat?"

"You're problem is you don't give a guy *anything*."

"And yours is you don't hold anything back."

"Well, I still think you're wrong about Ethan."

"Come on, Ems. I mean look at Joel."

Emily had seen Joel a few times.

"Okay. You might be right about Joel. But he's just his partner."

"Exactly."

Emily took a moment to get what Morgan meant. Partner didn't mean business partner.

"Oh," Emily said at last. They took their usual shortcut through the empty lot where a mom-and-pop convenience store had been when they were girls. These days it was a shrub-filled tangle far back from the streetlights. The shortcut was the darkest part of the walk home. For a while now, Emily had had the feeling that they were being watched. Occasionally, as they walked, she had glanced over her shoulder, but had seen no one around. She shrugged it off. After all, this was her street, one of the safest neighbourhoods in the city.

As they walked through the darkness of the empty lot, the feeling that they were being followed returned and Emily once more checked over her shoulder. She started to walk a little faster, Morgan keeping up, chattering away. They crossed the empty lot and were back on a well-lit street, their street. It was only a block or so to her house. Morgan sucked noisily at the last froth at the bottom of her cup, trying to get every bit of her mocha. Just like her, Emily thought. Satisfied, Morgan tossed her empty cup at someone's garbage can, missing it.

"You are such a slob," Emily said, stopping to pick up the cup and place it in the trash.

"Yeah, but I'm a sexually-fulfilled slob."

"Well then you won't mind if I keep Daniel. I mean, with all the guys you can have, why bother with a skinny, dorky guy?"

"Good point," Morgan said.

"However," Emily continued, "you know, there is one guy I wouldn't mind if you took."

She looked over at Morgan, grinning. Morgan grabbed her arm, laughing.

"Don't even say it! He is so gross!"

"He likes to give gifts. And look at the way he dresses. All that retro stuff you like."

"His clothes are beyond retro. They're dumpster-dives!"

Emily laughed. "Dumpster-dives? Did you make that up?"

"Michael is a creep, and you should stay as far away from him as possible."

"It's kind of hard to when we work at the same place."

"Maybe not for much longer. Did you see the way Ethan talked to him?"

"Yeah! I couldn't believe it. Ethan was actually tough with Michael."

"Yeah. Nothing neat about Ethan that time," Morgan said.

They had reached Morgan's house. The lights were out, her parents obviously already in bed. Morgan opened the front gate and stepped into her yard. She stopped and turned to look at her friend. She was suddenly serious.

"You are just too nice to people, Ems. Someday one'll turn around and bite you on the ass."

"Maybe. I'll take my chances until then."

Morgan shook her head and smiled. Emily waved and walked away.

"See ya," she said. Morgan waved back.

"Night. And hey, if this Daniel guy e-mails you, and you actually respond, I want to know everything. Got it?"

"Got it," Emily replied, giving her friend a little salute.

"And," Morgan shouted as Emily got farther away. "If he doesn't e-mail you, don't worry about it. It just means he's neat!"

"Good night, Morgan!" Emily shouted back.

Emily walked across the street, grinning, suddenly hoping that there would be an e-mail waiting when she got home. As she neared her gate, the feeling that she was being watched returned. She picked up her pace a little, glancing over her shoulder, still not seeing anyone. It upset her, feeling like this on her own street.

The house she had grown up in was a large, drafty, Victorian-style home built early in the last century, and unlike Morgan's, nearly every light in her house was on. As she ran up the steps and opened the front doors, she smelled coffee brewing and heard the sound of Miles Davis playing softly on the living room stereo.

She hung up her purse and jacket on the rack mounted on the wall just inside the front door. She heard her parents' voices from the direction of the kitchen.

"Hi, guys. I'm home."

Chapter 7

There was an e-mail from Daniel waiting when Emily logged on at 10:47, almost an hour after her shift at the Cyber Taste had ended. Daniel's e-mail had arrived at 10:07. It read:

> Hi Emily,
> Hope this isn't too quick. I really wanted to talk to you. And I wanted to make sure you had gave me youre real e-mail address. (Ha Ha) or (LOL) or whatever your supossed to type to show your just kidding. Please get back to me when you can.
> Daniel

Emily smiled at the note, and couldn't help but notice the typos. Guess he was in too much of a rush to do a spell-check, she thought. She placed a glass of water on the blue mat that covered her little computer desk and hit the reply button.

> Hi, Daniel!
> I didn't think you would e-mail me this fast! I guess I must be a pretty good waitress to make such a good impression (LOL). I suppose you're probably in bed by now (like you said it is a school night!) Why don't you e-mail me tomorrow? I should be home about 4:30. Looking forward to it!
>> Bye for now,
>> Emily.

She looked it over, perhaps a little too many exclamation points. Did it make her look like a silly schoolgirl and not the sophisticated, intelligent person she wanted him to think she was? The grammar was a little shaky but the spelling was perfect. She didn't even have to use her spell checker.

Emily stopped worrying and hit send. She took a sip of water and began to stand when she heard the familiar bleep sound, telling her there was new mail. She looked at the subject line: FRIEND-SHIP.

> Hi again!
> Great to here from you! And so fast too! I was still up so I thought Id send a reply before you went to bed. Do you want to stay

up and talk? I mean, wright or whatever!
Daniel

Emily read the e-mail twice. He must have typed it very quickly. She started to reply and noticed her heart was racing as fast as her fingertips.

Hi again, again!
You are pretty eager to talk aren't you? I apologize again for tonight. It was so busy! Usually on Tuesdays we are totally bored. Of course the one time I actually want to talk to someone, it goes crazy in there. Good for tips, though. Speaking of which, you ran off without giving me one! Not very nice.
Emily (the poor working girl)

Another bleep followed a minute later.

HI!
I know! I realized what I did when we were half-way home! I wanted to go back, but Jamie told me to forget it. It was his car, so what could I do? I promise I will tip you the very next time I see you. I will be seeing you again, right?
Daniel
(p.s. Jamie's the blonde guy, the loud one)

She typed:

Hi

Well, it is a coffee shop. I can't keep you out, can I? Don't worry about the tip. The service sucked tonight anyway. I was ignoring you because you were so rude to me at the beginning. You should be nicer to waitresses.

Emily

Emily hesitated, her finger over the send button. Did she really want to say that the service sucked? Was there a better expression? She decided to stop worrying so much. He was in no position to criticize her language skills.

Hi,

Me rude? When? Maybe at first because the guys were riding me all the way down their. You know how it is. And what I meant was I wanted to see you some place other than work. It makes it hard to get to know someone when they're running off every five seconds.

Daniel

If she didn't know better, she would have guessed he had been talking to Morgan. It was almost exactly what she had said on the walk home.

Hi,

What makes you think I want to be known better? Maybe I'm just nice to you

because I want a good tip.
    Emily

    Hi,
    Well that didn't work for you tonight, did it? Look I'm serious. We should get together sometime. How about this weekend? We could go see a movie or something?
    Daniel

    Hi,
    Not so fast. I don't date strange boys. Let's do this for a while and see what happens.
    Emily

They went back and forth like that for about fifteen minutes before Daniel suggested they go on a chat line. It was supposed to be faster and a better way to talk on-line. Emily thought about that for a moment, but in the end declined, saying that it was getting way too late. She sent the last e-mail, telling him to contact her tomorrow after school, and that she would let him know what she wanted to do next.

She stood up and yawned. Glancing at the clock on the nightstand next to her single bed she saw that it was past midnight. She grinned and shook her head and started to walk over to her bed, hoping that she would fall asleep, and not lie awake thinking of Daniel.

Her computer bleeped again and she turned to

look at it. The subject line read: FRIENDSHIP.

Emily shook her head. "Daniel!" she said softly to the empty room. Instead of sitting, she leaned over the keyboard and opened the latest message.

Hi,

I wanted to apologize for my behaviour this evening. I hope you know that I was just being my old jealous self. And I am sorry if I said anything to upset you. I had to let you know how I felt right away. After all, honesty is the core of our relationship, right?

As I told you, I have a great surprise that will be ready by next Friday. By the way, I know it's late, but if you are still up, maybe you could reply. I don't think I could sleep without knowing I was forgiven for acting like a jerk!

Love always,
Michael

Emily stopped leaning over the keyboard and sat down again, fully awake now. She hit the reply button. Maybe if he saw it in writing he would finally get the idea; at least she hoped he would.

Hi,

I want you to understand that you have to listen when I tell you things. Like no more presents and not to get too personal. People have to have boundaries. If you want to be friends (and only friends) then stop giving me gifts. Also, I don't know what you have planned for next Friday, but I would prefer if you didn't do anything.

Emily

She hit the send button and walked back to her bed, lying down heavily. The computer bleeped. She ignored it. It bleeped again. After the fifth message, she got up and walked over to the desk and shut down the computer. She'd had enough for one night.

Chapter 8

The bells rang, signalling the end of the school day. Emily sighed and packed up her books, putting them carefully back in the proper spots in her backpack. The last class had been Math and the teacher was telling them not to forget their assignment, and by the way, have a great weekend. Emily was only half-listening.

She was just glad the weekend was finally here and that Friday had come and gone with no sign of Michael. She hadn't received any more of those disturbing, personal e-mails from him either. She hoped that it meant he had finally got the message. Every time he had tried to approach her during that week, either at work or school, she had managed to brush him off or avoid him altogether.

Daniel was another matter.

They had e-mailed back and forth every day since the first time last Tuesday. She loved his sense of humour and how sweet he seemed in his little notes. He had come to the café as often as he could, even spending practically the whole day there on Sunday. She had even let him walk her home — with Morgan tagging along, of course. They had talked often on the phone and she had agreed to see him tomorrow after her shift. He asked her what she wanted to do.

"Anything but go for coffee," she said and heard him laugh.

"Okay," he had replied. "I think I can come up with something more original."

As Emily descended the stairs from the second level, she saw Morgan waiting at the lockers.

"Ready?" Morgan asked.

"What a day!" Emily said. "I thought it'd never end. At least I didn't get any surprises from Michael."

They started to walk down the hall toward the main exit, pushing past the crowds of kids rushing to get free for the weekend.

"I saw LaCreep at lunch, sitting in the corner of the lunchroom, staring at you with this weird smile on his face."

LaCreep was Morgan's new name for Michael LaVide. Emily just shook her head. Michael staring at her was nothing new. As they walked down the front steps, they heard excited shouts and saw kids running to the south side of the school.

"What's going on?" Morgan asked.

"Let's go see," Emily replied.

They followed the crowd and before they rounded the corner of the building they saw a huge plume of black smoke rising from the parking area. A heavy odour of gasoline hung in the air. As they turned the corner, they could see the source of the smoke. A car was on fire in the students' area and through the flames and the thick smoke, Emily knew there was something familiar about it.

"Did someone set a teacher's car on fire?" Morgan asked, grinning at the idea.

"It's the student lot," Emily replied. As she spoke, more kids rushed by, trying to get as close to the burning car as they could. She heard someone shout something about getting marshmallows to toast. Emily saw most of the kids around the car had this odd gleeful look.

Then she saw Justin being held back by his friends, stopping him from running toward the burning vehicle. He was screaming, swearing loudly as he watched his precious car literally go up in smoke. Morgan put a hand over her mouth, astonished. Then she laughed.

"I don't believe it!" she said, turning to Emily. "Finally he gets some payback."

Emily turned away, afraid of the way she felt — the pure joy that filled her in watching him suffer. It had been so long since she and Justin had been together, but deep in some dark part of her it felt good to watch him suffer.

"Who would do that?" Morgan asked as they

walked away, glancing over her shoulder to watch the scene. They both could hear the sound of sirens getting closer.

"How do I know?" Emily replied. "Maybe there was something wrong with the engine."

"Something wrong?" Morgan said. "Ems, cars don't just blow up!"

"What, are you an expert on cars?" Emily asked.

"Well," Morgan replied, nudging her and grinning, "the back seat anyway."

"Oh, gross!" Emily said.

As they left the school property, Emily looked across the street toward the park. Michael stood by the bench in the shade of a huge oak, smiling at her. She grabbed Morgan's shoulder, stopping her. Her heart leapt into her throat and she turned her back to the park.

"What?" Morgan asked

"He's there!" she said.

"Who?"

Emily indicated the park over her shoulder.

"There's no one there, Ems," Morgan said.

Emily turned back around. The spot under the oak was empty.

Chapter 9

Emily ran up the stairs to her front door and rushed inside.

"I'm home!" she shouted toward the kitchen. As usual, she could hear music playing softly and smell the coffee her parents were constantly brewing. Her Saturday shift at the Cyber Taste had gone a little longer than normal because of the crowd. She was supposed to meet Daniel at seven, which left her less than forty-five minutes to get ready and get downtown.

She tossed her things onto the coat rack and ran upstairs to her room. Inside, she pulled off her shirt and scrambled around trying to find the outfit she had planned to wear on their first official date. She had been up too late talking to Daniel on the phone and had slept in, so she hadn't laid out clothes for the evening as she had planned.

Emily had formed a new plan on her mad rush

home. First, find something to wear. Second, take the world's fastest shower. Third, bug one of her parents to give her a ride downtown since there was no way she would make it on time by bus.

Emily opened her dresser drawer, tossing items aside in a frantic search for the camisole she had wanted to wear. It was always the way: the one thing you're looking for in a rush you can never find. Now that she thought about it, there were a few things missing, things she hadn't seen for a couple of weeks. She would check with Morgan, to make sure she hadn't borrowed her stuff without asking again.

Her mother stepped into the room.

"Hi, honey. I thought I heard you."

"Hi, Mom. Look I'm supposed to meet someone downtown in less than an hour. Could you drive me?"

"Who are you meeting?"

"Just a friend. Could you?"

"I suppose. Is this someone we know?"

Emily stopped her frantic search for clothes and turned to look at her mother. It had been a long time since she had gone on a date, and she had deliberately not mentioned Daniel to her mother. Her parents still worried about her.

"Mom, look. It's a guy. Someone I met at the café."

Her mother came into the room, arms folded across her chest, looking very serious. Emily waited tensely for her mother's words, not knowing how she would react.

"Well," she said at last, her expression warming, "congratulations!"

"What?"

"It's about time! Your father and I were wondering when you would finally start dating again."

Emily was shocked. "You mean you don't mind?"

"Why would I mind? It's normal for a girl your age to go on dates. What isn't normal is for you to be working all the time and spending every weekend alone."

Emily gave her head a confused shake. Parents.

"Look. I'll just have a quick shower, and then could you drive me? We're meeting across from City Hall at seven."

"That's not leaving you much time."

"That's why I'm rushing, Mom."

"Well, maybe you should call this Daniel. Ask him to come over here tonight."

"You have got to be kidding!"

"I'm serious. What's wrong with him coming over to the house?"

"Mother! Did I mention that this was a guy, *and* it's the first time we're doing something together?" Emily watched as her mother stood there considering this. "And I'd really like this not to be the last time I see him?"

"I still don't see what's wrong with him coming over here."

Emily glanced at her watch.

"For one thing, it's too late to call him. I'm supposed to meet him in forty minutes," she paused for effect. "For another, there's no better way to get rid of a guy than to have him spend Saturday night with your parents. He'll think I'm a total loser!"

"So now you're an expert on the opposite sex?"

"I know that much."

"We're not that bad," her mother replied. "Some of your friends actually like hanging out with us."

"Once again. Can you drive me?" Emily asked, hoping to change the subject.

"Alright. Just make sure you're home by curfew."

"Whatever!" Emily said as she headed down the hall to shower.

* * *

Emily glanced at the clock on the dash of her parent's old Volvo. She had less than ten minutes to get to City Hall. She tapped her foot against the floorboards as her mother made a slow, deliberate U-turn at the bottom of their street and headed north on the main road.

As they drove past the empty lot at the end of their street, Emily saw someone standing perfectly still just at its edge. As the car slipped past him, she recognized the stooped shoulders, the faded army surplus jacket.

Michael made no effort to hide, he stared directly at her as she drove past.

Chapter 10

Daniel had promised her an original experience, and this definitely qualified.

"Are you sure we're allowed in here?" Emily asked as they walked up to the front doors of a tiny club. She had heard of the place before, of course. Her parents came here often. The neon sign over the door read "Baby Blues."

"Relax," Daniel replied. "They know me here."

She found it hard to believe that someone their age would be known in a place like this, but they had walked in without anyone saying a word. They were escorted to a great table just a few feet from the stage. As she looked around, she saw that they were easily the youngest people in the place. At least that's what she assumed as she looked at the crowd through the smoky haze filling the club. At first she felt odd and out of place in the dark room filled with adults ordering drinks, talking, and laughing loudly. She and Daniel sat close together to hear each other over the noise. After a while, she felt herself relax a little.

As they sat there, a compact, heavily built man walked over to their table. He wore an unusually shiny black suit and sunglasses and Emily wondered how he could see in the dark room. Daniel stood up as the man approached and they gripped hands and patted each other on the shoulder.

"Hey! You're looking good, Manny!" Daniel shouted over the crowd and the sound of blues music playing softly on the speakers. "For an old guy, I mean."

Manny gave him a look and faked a jab at Daniel's belly. Daniel covered up a moment too late and laughed. "The old guy's still faster than you," Manny grinned and then looked down at Emily, smiling at her.

"And who's this young lady?" he asked. Daniel turned and smiled down at her.

"This is Emily Taylor. Emily, this is my uncle Manny. He owns this place."

The older man bowed slightly and reached out his hand. Emily took it and they shook, Manny placed his left hand over hers gently. She noticed the huge diamond ring on his pinkie, the carefully manicured fingers and how soft his hand was.

"Charmed," Manny said. "And I don't own the place, really, I'm just one of the partners."

"Hi," was all Emily could think to respond.

"Manny's the reason people come to this joint,"

Daniel said with obvious pride, as he sat back down beside her. "He's one of the best blues guitar men in the world."

Manny laughed and put a hand on Daniel's shoulder. "He exaggerates, Emily. I'm hardly the best in the world. Maybe in the West, though." Then he laughed again, a thick, smoky laugh that Emily found pleasant.

"Danny here is coming along as well. He might be better than me one day."

Daniel grinned at her, and even in the dim light she saw he was blushing.

"You play guitar?" Emily asked, stunned.

"Yeah," Daniel said.

"Why didn't you tell me?"

He shrugged. "It never came up."

"You told me you liked blues, but you didn't say you played."

"He's just pretending to be bashful, Emily." Manny said. "He knows he's good. After all, he had a great teacher. Me!"

"Do you know the blues?" Manny asked her.

"A little," she said. "I like Chicago blues. You know, guys like Willie Dixon and Elmore James. I love Koko Taylor's voice."

Emily tried to smile as she saw Manny's eyebrows rise over the dark glasses. Even Daniel looked surprised. Then Manny cuffed his nephew on the shoulder.

"You better hold on to this one," he said. He smiled at her and began to leave, explaining he had to get ready to perform.

"Wow. I had no idea you were so into the blues!" Daniel said.

She smiled and sipped her cranberry and soda. "My parents are both music teachers and play all kinds of stuff at home. I guess some of it stuck," she said. "My folks always make me keep an open mind."

Daniel seemed impressed.

"I hardly ever listen to the stuff on the radio," he said. "It's all too commercial."

"I know," Emily replied.

There was a pause.

"So both your parents are music teachers, huh? So what do you play?"

"Piano and the recorder. And I'm bad at both. My parents didn't pass along the music gene I guess."

"I bet you're good."

Emily ducked her head to sip her drink. She didn't know how to react to his comment. A part of her wondered if he really meant it, or if he was just being polite.

"Are you going to play tonight?"

"Me? Here?" he sounded shocked. "No way. I'm not ready for a place like this yet. I'll stick to my basement."

"You have to come out sometime," she said. Then she had an inspiration. "I know! Why don't you play at the Café? I bet I can arrange it with Ethan."

He laughed. "So you're my manager now?"

"Sure. Does it pay? I do have to come up with my tuition, you know."

"Tuition? For what?"

"For university, what else?"

"Oh," he said. He took a sip of his Coke. "Are you going to stay in Calgary?"

She sipped her own drink and shook her head. "No. I'm going to Vancouver."

"Oh," he said. "Why not stay here?"

"I want to study film, and the school in Vancouver's one of the best."

He nodded. "Film, huh. That's pretty cool."

"What I really want to do is travel for a while," Emily said. This guy was so easy to talk to. "But my parents want me to get an education first."

"Oh, yeah? Where do you want to travel?"

"I don't know. Europe, I guess. Greece, maybe, and the south of France."

"You like the warmth?"

"I did grow up in Canada. I've kind of done the cold thing. So what about you? What are you going to do after school?"

"I don't know. Get a day job, I guess. Maybe play guitar nights."

"Is that what you want to be? A musician?"

"I already am a musician," he said, grinning. "I just want to get paid doing it."

"Cool," she said, wishing she had that kind of confidence. Emily saw movement on the stage, the musicians starting to take their positions.

Manny came on last and he nodded down at them through the applause. Daniel stood and turned his chair to face the stage better. He also moved closer to her, their knees touching as he slipped his hand over the back of her chair. Emily realized that she didn't mind him sitting so close to her. In fact, it was really nice. The musicians finished tuning their instruments and checking their microphones. She felt his hand slip gently off her chair and on to her shoulder. Her first impulse was to sit forward and let his hand fall away. Then she stopped herself. Look at me, Emily thought, out on a real date!

"Wait till you hear this," Daniel said as the music began.

* * *

As they walked slowly down the sidewalk, a light snow began to fall. They stopped and looked up at the falling flakes illuminated by the streetlights. The only sounds were coming from the cars speeding by on Eighth Street. After a few minutes, they stopped looking at the sky and looked at each other. Daniel took his hand out of his pocket and raised it to her face. Instinctively, she snapped her head back, startled by his sudden movement.

"What?" he said as he quickly lowered his hand.

She shook her head. "Sorry. I guess you startled me."

"Did something happen to you?"

She was shaken by the question. What did he know?

"What do you mean?"

He shrugged, shoving his hands back into the pockets of his jacket. "You don't trust people easily."

"Is it that obvious?"

He laughed, and so did she.

"I guess that was a dumb question, huh? Just be patient, okay?" she asked and Daniel nodded. There was a sudden gust of wind and the snow fell heavier now.

"We better get going, you'll miss the bus."

It was a little warmer inside the bus shelter; the glass protected them from the wind. They stood in silence, and Daniel looked across the street, his hands still in his pockets.

"I had fun tonight," she said at last.

Daniel looked at her, smiling. "Oh, yeah? Well, I'm glad. I was hoping it would be fun."

There was another awkward moment of silence and Emily looked past his shoulder to see if the bus was approaching.

"It's too bad you have to be home so early."

"My parents are pretty cool. But they are strict about curfew. Especially if I'm out with a boy."

"How come? Are you out with boys a lot?"

She laughed. "Not much. Not for a while anyway."

"Are they just strict or are they worried about you meeting some strange guy?"

"Both."

"I'm not strange, am I?"

"Not so far. It's early in the relationship, though."

"The relationship?" he said, smiling.

"Well, we have known each other for a month or so now. So I guess we've had a platonic relationship, right?"

"Right," he said. "What is platonic anyway? Another word for boring?"

Emily pushed away from him slightly. "Oh? So now I'm boring am I?"

"No. I'll let you know when I'm bored."

"I bet you will," Emily replied.

They were standing close enough that she saw their breath merging in the cool night air. He took his hands out of his pockets again, staring into her eyes.

"Can I try this again?"

She nodded. Daniel leaned forward to kiss her. She let his lips touch hers and then stepped back, turning her head slightly away. She had felt more and more comfortable with him as the evening progressed, but there was something about this moment that frightened her, a memory of Justin, standing too close, looming over her. Daniel looked a little hurt.

"Sorry," she said quickly. "It's not you. I just need to take things slow."

Then the bus came and they stepped out of the shelter. As the door opened, they said their good-nights and she saw that Daniel was still a little upset by her reaction to his kiss. Impulsively, she grabbed his coat and pulled him close, giving him a quick kiss on the lips.

"See ya!" she shouted as she jumped on the bus, the doors sliding shut. She was smiling as she ran to the back and found a seat. She was amazed at her own act of bravery.

* * *

Emily was still smiling as she walked down her street, thinking about the evening, about Daniel. Her thoughts were interrupted by the sound of a loud engine rumbling, getting louder as it approached down the street behind her. She turned to look and saw a bright orange two-door car stop in front of Morgan's house. The passenger door swung open and Emily heard a sudden blast of hip-hop and saw who was in the passenger seat. She rolled her eyes and waited, leaning against her fence. Morgan finally jumped out of the car, laughing as the driver tried to grab her one last time.

"Watch the hands, pal," she shouted as she turned to slam the door shut. The car took off with a squeal of tires. Lights flashed on upstairs in the house next door.

"That was pure class," Emily said as she walked over to join her friend.

"Ems!" Morgan said. "What are you doing out

here? Looking for pointers?"

"As if! I just got home from my date."

Morgan's eyes lit up. "That's right!" she laughed, wrapping an arm around Emily. "So how was it? Tell me everything!"

She leaned close and sniffed Emily's clothes.

"You suddenly take up smoking?"

"Is it that bad?" She and Daniel had practically been the only ones not smoking in the club.

Morgan nodded. "Where did you go?"

"We went to a blues club downtown."

Morgan nodded. "Wow. That does sound exciting," she said, not the least bit excited.

"There's more."

"Oh, well! Let's get started."

Emily opened her gate and they ran up the steps to the house. As usual, her parents were at the rear of the house in the kitchen, music playing on the stereo. Her parents were not into material things. They didn't spend money on fancy clothes and their car was almost as old as Emily. But the stereo was top of the line and their music collection was huge and just as varied as any library. They had also spent a lot of money on the kitchen and its sunroom. As Emily entered the kitchen, her parents were sitting at the island, going over schoolwork.

"Hi, guys," Emily said. Both her parents jumped a little, startled by the sudden intrusion.

"Hi, girls," her dad said. "We didn't hear you come in."

"You two really have to start locking the doors. Anyone could just walk in on you," Morgan said. It was something she had said many times before.

Emily's mother smiled at her. "When we have to lock the door to feel safe, then it's time to move." It was her standard answer.

"We're going upstairs for a while," Emily said, grabbing Morgan by the arm.

"Wait!" her mother called to her. "How was the date?"

"It was nice."

"Nice?" her mother asked. "That's all you're going to say?"

Emily waved and headed back down the hall toward the stairs.

"Don't worry Mrs T. I'll get all the info for you!" Morgan shouted back.

"I'm counting on it," Emily's mother shouted back.

Upstairs, Morgan jumped on the bed, leaning back against the headboard. She grabbed one of Emily's pillows and hugged it as she waited. Emily stood at the foot of her bed.

"So?" Morgan said at last. "How did it go?"

Emily smiled. "It was really nice." She knew Morgan waited for details, but she kept silent.

"So tell me!" Morgan shouted, throwing the pillow at her.

Emily sat on the bed and started to tell her about the evening. Morgan kept pressing for more details, but there weren't that many. Not the kind

Morgan was hoping for, at least.

"He did kiss you good night, right?"

"Sure." Emily replied.

"And you let him. Right?"

"A bit."

Morgan groaned. "Would you get over yourself! Give the guy a chance."

"I will. Next time. So what did you do tonight?" She wanted to change the subject. Just then, as if on cue, her computer bleeped indicating new mail. Emily ignored it.

"Do you want to get that?" Morgan asked.

"It can wait," Emily said casually. She hoped it was from Daniel, but knew it could easily be from Michael.

Morgan saw right through her but changed the subject anyway. She started to tell her about the party she'd been at. The main topic of conversation at the party had been Justin's car blowing up yesterday.

"Did anyone know what happened?" Emily asked.

"Supposedly the fire department is investigating. I guess they think it was set deliberately."

"Who would do something like that?" Emily asked.

"You mean besides you?" Morgan said grinning.

"Now? Like two years later?"

"Maybe you were waiting for the right time to plot your revenge."

Emily just shook her head. "I'm serious. Why would someone do that to Justin?"

"Look, we're not the only ones in school who can't stand the guy. It's just too bad he wasn't in it."

"God, Morgan! That's terrible!"

"Come on! Like you haven't wished worse on him."

Emily touched her upper arm, as if the bruises were still there.

* * *

Justin had been her first crush and her first boyfriend. She had been so naïve back then, not knowing what to expect in a relationship. At first he had been great, very caring, always complimenting her. He was a year older and already had a car and they would take long drives just to talk and be together. Soon, the car rides became an excuse to park somewhere secluded. Each time he kept pushing her to let things go further. Emily always resisted. During the first couple of weeks he was a gentleman, but that wore off. She began to dread being alone in the car with him, and when she didn't let him touch her, he hit her. The blows were always in places no one would be able to see easily. Once or twice her mother or Morgan would see the bruises, but she would lie and say she'd had an accident, or that it happened in gym class. She was too humiliated to tell even her best friend.

In the spring, Justin planned a huge party at his place. His parents were going out of town that weekend. Morgan had shown up with some football player, one even older than Justin. By the evening of the party, Emily dreaded ever being alone with Justin. He had started drinking early and later had tried to lead her up to his room several times. Eventually, of course, she could no longer fight his attempts to get her alone upstairs. He was rougher than usual with her, and the stink of alcohol on his breath nauseated her. She fought him off this time, no longer able to put up with the humiliation. When he started to tear at her clothes, she screamed. The first to arrive had been Morgan and her date. The football player picked Justin up and tossed him across the room. Emily told him to leave Justin alone. All she wanted to do was get out. Morgan grabbed a blanket and wrapped it around Emily as they ran out of the house.

Next week the rumours began in school. Justin started spreading all these lies about her, about what they did when they were alone. Strange boys started calling her up, making horrible suggestions. She wished that she hadn't stopped the football player from hurting him. Emily hadn't told anyone, hadn't called the police even though Morgan begged her to. The only other person she had told was her mother.

* * *

The computer bleeped several more times in quick succession.

"Are you going to keep ignoring that?" Morgan asked at last.

"I'll get it later."

Morgan jumped off the bed. "Let's look now! Maybe lover boy's sending you messages, telling you how wonderful the evening was!"

Emily jumped over to stop her, but wasn't fast enough. Morgan hit the mouse and the screen sprang to life.

"There's a lot here," Morgan said, scanning the inbox. "Daniel's been busy. Let's see, it says "friendship." That's gotta be him, right?"

"Leave it, Morgan!" Emily said, trying to grab the mouse from her. "It's private."

"Oh please! Like you can keep secrets from me."

She opened one and started to read, giggling a little at the note. Emily sighed and waited until she got to the end, reading the signature at the bottom. Love always, Michael. Morgan turned to Emily, open-mouthed.

"What the hell is going on here?"

Emily said nothing. She felt really embarrassed now.

"I thought you told him to leave you alone?"

"I did. He stopped for a while, then he started up again. I don't even read them anymore," Emily lied. In fact, she had read all of them, partly from curiosity, to see how his little fantasy relationship was progressing.

"Is this all he's been doing?"

Emily shrugged.

"What else?"

"Well. He's dropped off some cards."

"He's come to the house?" Morgan asked, shocked.

"He's never been inside. He leaves them in the mailbox."

"Let's see them," Morgan demanded, holding out her hand.

Emily reached under her bed and pulled out the shoebox where she kept printouts of the e-mails as well as the handmade cards Michael had given her. Morgan's eyes grew wide at the thick pile of letters and the pale blue envelopes. She grabbed one and pulled out the card. Again, there was a beautiful photograph of Emily on the cover and inside was a long, rambling letter written in his precise script, covering every inch of space. The cards and e-mails were peppered with bits of poems and song lyrics (complete with piano chords) all of which he claimed he had written because her love had inspired him.

The two girls sat on the floor, backs leaning against Emily's bed as they went through them. Morgan was freaked out at first, but began to laugh or, occasionally, groan at some of the more syrupy lines.

"I know he's a freak," Emily said. "But it is kind of flattering to have a guy like you so much. I mean, who wouldn't want a guy to write poems and songs about you."

"Oh, get lost!" Morgan shouted. "He's a psycho! You should burn this stuff."

"I know. But I feel sorry for him. I just think I should hold on to it. In case."

"In case of what?" Morgan asked. "He becomes a famous psycho?"

Emily couldn't put into words how she felt. She was mixed up inside. Michael's attention was flattering *because* she knew that there was no chance of it ever developing into a relationship. Creepy as he could be, there was something about knowing there was someone out there who thought of her this way.

Morgan shook her head. "Man! Both of you need to get some help."

To lighten up things, Emily grabbed one of her favourites and looked through it for the part she liked.

"Listen to this," she said, starting to read out loud. "What have I become, my sweetest friend? Everyone I know goes away in the end." She looked at Morgan. "Isn't that so sad?"

"Nine Inch Nails," Morgan said.

"What?"

"That's who wrote that. The rest of it goes: 'I will let you down, I will make you hurt.' It isn't sweet, it's a threat."

Emily felt a little sick. "He didn't write this?"

Morgan looked through the printouts. "As far as I can see, he stole all of it." She picked up a printout at random. "'The pearl inside your heart.'

That's Ricky Lee Jones." She read some more. "'You can make the mountains ring or the angels cry.' That's some song from the sixties. And this," she said, reading another line, "'I don't mind what happens now and then, as long as you be my friend in the end.'" She looked at Emily.

"That's a song by 3 Doors Down." She looked through them all. "Warren Zevon. Foo Fighters. All of this is ripped off."

"Are you sure?"

"There's a lot more music out there than Britney Spears and that jazz crap your parents make you listen to."

Emily looked at the e-mails again, disappointed now. It had felt better when she thought her secret admirer was at least a poet. Morgan was still looking at the printouts. She seemed to notice something else.

"Did you read this one?" Morgan asked. Emily looked at it.

"What about it?" Some of the longer ones she had just skimmed. They tended to become repetitive.

"He's got this long description of the first time he saw you back in Grade 7. He goes on and on about your red hair and green eyes."

"What? Let me see that!"

Morgan handed her the letter and Emily read it. Michael described how he had first seen her in the school cafeteria, how light seemed to flow from her. He wrote a long description of her strawberry-red hair, her green-gold eyes.

93

"That is too bizarre! Has he even looked at me?" Her hair was auburn, its slight reddish tint more obvious in the summer. Emily's eyes were a dark green. "This guy is even weirder than I thought. He thinks he's in love with you and he doesn't even have a clue what you look like."

Emily read the passage again. What was going on? Why did he see her this way? Was he perhaps describing some other girl?

"Maybe he just sees me the way he wishes I was."

"I am so serious," Morgan said at last. "Burn all this stuff!"

Emily nodded, looking down at the pile of papers surrounding them.

"You're right. I should get rid of it."

"Let's go downstairs and get a fire going." Morgan stood up, excited by her brilliant idea.

Part of Emily thought it was a great idea, another part of her wasn't so sure. She picked up the print-outs and tossed them back into the shoebox.

"What now?" Morgan asked, seeing her hesitate.

"I don't know. I just think I should hold onto it in case I need it later. You know, if he starts acting even more weird."

Morgan sighed, seeing that Emily wasn't going to burn the letters.

"Fine! Whatever! Keep them if it gives you a thrill. But listen to me. Tell LaFreak to leave you alone. Permanently!"

Chapter 11

"Have you seen Michael?" Ethan asked Emily as she and Morgan were getting ready for their shift.

"Why are you asking me?" Emily replied.

He was at his usual high wooden stool behind the register and held the telephone receiver in his hand. "I've been trying to get hold of him. Two of the computers are acting up and I can't reach him. I thought since you two were so close, you might know where he was."

Emily was tired of all the jokes about her and Michael. She just walked past Ethan to get her apron from the storage room.

"I guess he must have written his number down wrong when he filled out his application. I tried it a couple of times and I get the weather info line."

"That figures," Morgan said. "This is the first time you've called him?"

"He's always here." Ethan shrugged.

Morgan chuckled. "Not always. He spends a lot of time sending e-mails."

"Morgan!" Emily replied. "You promised!"

"Promised what?" Ethan asked, intrigued, noticing the look Emily gave Morgan.

"Don't mind her," Morgan said as she followed Emily behind the counter. "She's so popular these days. Two guys are after her!"

Ethan sat up straight on the stool. He loved gossip.

"Really? Well, we all know about our computer guy, but who's the other one?"

"Come on, guys. Do I have to tell everyone about this?" Emily said, exasperated. She slipped her apron over her head and then handed Morgan hers.

"Emily went on a date last night with this guy she met here."

"Oh, no, he's a customer?" Ethan said, abruptly looking very serious.

"Yeah," Morgan replied, looking over at Emily, puzzled by his reaction.

"I'm sorry. But we have a strict rule here at the Cyber Taste. No dating customers. I guess you're going to have to give him up or quit."

The girls' looked at each other in stunned silence. Then Ethan started to laugh.

"Got ya!" he said, laughing even harder. "That was too easy."

The girls grinned and Morgan gave him a little shove. "That was so mean!" she exclaimed.

"Imagine it was a rule!" he said. "I'd never meet anyone! So, last night was the first date. How did it go?"

"It was nice," she replied. Telling Morgan was one thing, but telling Ethan about her date seemed a bit bizarre.

"Details, I want details."

"Why do you want to know so badly? It was just a typical teenage date."

"Well," Ethan said, sighing. "When you get to my age, you have to live vicariously through the young." He shook his head sadly.

Morgan had poured her first coffee and snorted at his little act.

"Please! I've seen you work the cute customers. It's a good thing Joel doesn't come by very much."

"What!" Ethan said, trying to look offended. Joel is just my business partner."

"Sure," Morgan replied.

Ethan raised his hands and shrugged. Emily walked over to the sink to wash up before her shift officially started. It was just after eight in the morning, the café's usual opening time on Sundays.

"Just tell me where you two went," Ethan said.

"I'm supposed to be working, remember?"

Ethan looked around. "Do you see anyone dying of thirst yet?"

"And we still have to drag the stupid board outside."

"Again," Ethan replied, "I must indicate the lack of customers at this juncture."

Giving up, she poured a coffee for herself and sat down behind the counter. She told him about the date last night, a much briefer version than she had related to Morgan.

"Now tell him what Michael's been up to," Morgan said.

Emily didn't want to tell anyone about that. Michael's delusion that he was having some kind of relationship was embarrassing, and being part of the high school rumour mill once before was quite enough for her. She didn't want to be attached to yet another freak. And now Morgan had shattered her silly schoolgirl illusions about how romantic Michael was trying to be.

Morgan nudged her on the arm. "Oh, tell him!"

"Oh, alright!" She topped up her mug, finding that she needed coffee after spending half the night talking with Morgan. She was glad that she only had a four hour shift today. Emily decided she wouldn't tell Ethan exactly how much Michael had been harassing her. The last thing she wanted was him losing his job and then blaming her. She had seen him angry, and didn't want it directed at her.

"You know about the gifts. Michael's also e-mailing me constantly, and giving me these cards he makes with these long, weird letters inside."

"What do the letters say?"

Morgan interrupted. "How they were meant to

be together. How great it is having a girlfriend like Emily."

"I thought this was my story?" Emily said.

Morgan held up her hands. "Oops! You're right. Carry on."

"Wait a minute," Ethan said. "He isn't trying to get you to be his girlfriend — he thinks you already are?"

Emily just nodded. Ethan looked aghast. "That is a bit bizarre, don't you think?"

"Tell me about it!" Morgan replied.

"What exactly has he been saying in these notes?" A serious tone had crept into his voice.

As she filled in the details for Ethan, Emily found that telling the story made it seem less and less creepy and more comical.

"He's obsessed with details. He tells me this useless trivia about karma and reincarnation and how we were together in past lives. He tells me about growing up and how his family was so perfect it was almost embarrassing. They even bought him a loft downtown for when he turns eighteen."

"A loft? So the parents are wealthy as well, I take it?"

"They probably just want to get rid of him," Morgan said. "If it's even true."

"Tell him about the code thing," Morgan went on.

Emily started to grin, thinking of Michael's proof they were meant to be together.

"Let me see if I can remember the details," Emily began. "It's got something to do with numerology. If you take our initials, Emily Taylor and Michael LaVide become E.T. and M.L., right? And then if you change them to a number by their place in the alphabet you get 5 and 20 for me and 13 and 12 for him. Got it?"

The other two just nodded, obviously lost.

"Okay. Then if you add them together, both equal 25. And then, 2 and 5 equal 7. That's the magic number, the number of lives we've lived. According to him, it's even the date of my birthday. Apparently, I was born on the seventh day of the seventh month."

"Were you?"

"Not even close."

Ethan shook his head. He seemed amazed at the depth of Michael's delusions.

"You don't seem too worried about all this," he said.

"I guess. It seems worse when you sit alone at night reading the notes he writes. But when you actually talk about it, it just seems silly."

She paused, thinking it over, and the others waited for a moment.

"What?" Ethan asked at last.

"The only thing that worries me a little is that he knows so much about me. Stuff like where I live and my parents' names. And how did he know my favourite flowers or about chocolate-covered orange peels?"

Ethan waved his hand dismissively. "He probably overheard you talking about flowers and things. And anyone could get your parents' names, either in the phone book or on one of those Internet directories. He *is* a computer geek. Who knows what he can find on the Internet? About any of us."

The bell over the door chimed as the first customers arrived.

"It's show time, ladies," Ethan said, standing up to smile at a group of four people who wandered in looking groggy.

"Let's get the sign out," Morgan said to Emily. As she stood, Ethan placed a hand on her shoulder.

"Look. You seem okay with this. But if it gets too much, or if you want me to deal with him, let me know."

She put her hand over his. "Thanks, Ethan. But I can handle it."

He looked at her with genuine concern and Emily found that she was touched by it.

"I'll take care of the sign this morning," he said.

"I'll do it," Emily said, "if you do me a favour."

Ethan looked suspicious. He knew how much they hated lugging the heavy sign outside. "What kind of favour?"

"Daniel is a musician. I promised him you'd let him play here."

"No," Ethan said. "Absolutely not. This is a

café, not a honky-tonk."

"What the hell is a honky-tonk?" Morgan blurted out.

Ethan and Emily ignored her.

"Come on," she pleaded. "Just one night a week. How about Tuesdays? They're always dead in here."

"Oh, and you want to scare off the rest the customers by having some teenage boy singing tunes from the *Best of Bread*?"

"What the hell is the *Best of Bread*?" Morgan piped up again.

"Just listen to him. If he's no good, then we forget the whole thing."

Ethan sighed. "Alright. First, he has to audition for Joel and I. If he's any good, then we'll see."

"How are you going to audition him?" Morgan said, and gave him a look. Ethan laughed.

"For one so young, you have a filthy mind. Keep it up."

Chapter 12

Emily was in the middle of placing an order when Michael finally showed up. She glanced at the clock over the door and saw that it was nearly eleven o'clock. Since the first few customers had dragged themselves in, it had been nearly nonstop in the café.

Michael seemed to be in a rather bad mood, and for the first time, seemed to be annoyed by Emily in particular. She didn't mind; it was actually nice to be left alone. She lost track of him as more customers arrived.

When it was close to noon, she began to clear up outstanding bills at her tables, glad her shift was over. Then, with a tray full of empty plates and mugs, she began to walk toward the counter. Suddenly, he was standing directly in front of her. Emily yelped as she nearly ran into him. Her tray tilted and a glass fell off, smashing on the tiled floor. A group of guys at a nearby table yelled and applauded her clumsiness. She crouched down to start picking up the pieces. Michael crouched down too, looking at her strangely.

"What's the matter? Guilty conscience?" he asked.

"What are you talking about?"

He didn't respond, and she couldn't make out what his vacant expression was supposed to mean. Or his comment. She started to pick up the shards of broken glass. Michael did too.

"Don't," she said curtly, "I can handle it."

"I want to help," he said. "Even though I caught you sneaking out last night."

His sudden appearance had given her a start, but now his comment angered her. She pushed his hands away as he tried to pick up the broken glass. She thought of what Morgan had told her. You had to be direct with a guy like Michael. He won't understand anything else. She remembered him skulking in the shadows on her street last night.

"Stay away from me! Stay away from my house!"

He smiled at her, that strange half-smile, now paired with the odd, vacant look in his eyes. She picked up the pieces and tossed them onto the tray. Standing, she brushed past Michael without looking or speaking to him.

"I know I was mad at you earlier," he said, following her. "But you know how I am. I get jealous sometimes, even though I know that musician guy means nothing to you. I understand, really. You were just being nice to him."

Emily spun around. She had only been annoyed before, but now rage filled her. She stood close to him, closer than she ever had before. To her surprise she began actually shouting at him.

"Don't ever talk to me again! Do you understand? Stay away from me!" she yelled. A woman turned around in her chair to look at her, but Emily kept going. I don't know where this stupid little fantasy of yours came from, and I don't care. Never speak to me again! Do you get it?" She was really screaming at him.

The café was silent now. Emily knew every eye was on her and she didn't care. She stood there glaring at Michael, waiting for some kind of response. But he just stared at her, blinking, as he always did when he was uncomfortable. She dropped her tray on the nearest table, not caring that it was occupied. Emily stepped even closer, their faces only inches apart.

"I asked you a question! Answer me!"

Michael nodded, all colour gone from his pale skin.

"Say it!" Emily said. "Tell me you know there's nothing between us!"

He smiled at that, and shook his head. "Come on, Ems …"

"Don't call me that!" she shouted. "You have no right to call me that!"

When he started to speak again, she cut him off,

"Say there's nothing between us! Say it!"

The smile was finally gone, and he nervously pushed his glasses off the bridge of his nose.

"There's nothing between us," he said flatly.

She pushed him away, feeling a little queasy as the adrenaline kept pumping through her bloodstream.

"Now get out of here!"

With that, she turned around and ran down the hall, pushing open the heavy fire door that led to the back alley. There was an old picnic table chained to a drainpipe for the staff to take their breaks, a garbage bin, and an overturned tin drum that served as an ashtray for the smokers.

Emily ran to the other side of the trash bin and bent over, retching. She felt terribly nauseous, but nothing came up. Instead, she leaned her cheek against the cool metal of the dumpster, trying to get her nerves back under control. She felt her legs shake and her knees start to buckle beneath her weight. Emily grabbed onto the edge of the dumpster for support.

She heard the door open and Morgan come out.

"Emily?" she called out, not seeing her behind the dumpster.

"Back here," she replied. Morgan stepped around the dumpster, looking pale and worried. Emily rushed toward her and they hugged.

"God! You're shaking," Morgan said at last, pulling away slightly to look at Emily. "Are you okay?"

"I don't think I've ever been that angry in my whole life," Emily said at last.

"He had it coming," Morgan said.

"But I lost it! In front of all those people. And Ethan! What will he think?"

"Relax. Ethan's on our side."

Morgan led Emily back to the picnic table and made her sit. Emily was still shaking as she ran her hand through her hair, pushing it from her eyes.

"Do you think he got it?"

Morgan grinned. "The whole neighbourhood got it, Ems."

Emily laughed, more as a reflex than from any humour she saw in the situation. She covered her face in her hands, and suddenly burst into tears. Morgan stroked Emily's hair, pushing it back from her face. She waited patiently as Emily tried to get her emotions back in check.

"Well, the shift's over now at least. You want me to get your stuff?"

"No. I'll go in with you."

"You sure?"

Emily nodded and stood up, wiping her eyes. She was glad not to be wearing any makeup today.

"How do I look?"

"Gorgeous," Morgan said. "Hell, I might start stalking you."

Emily laughed again, this time a real laugh. They walked back inside, arms around each other. A little apprehensive, Emily looked around, making sure Michael was gone.

"Don't worry," Morgan said. "He took off as soon as you ran outside."

Emily was glad to see that most of the customers who had witnessed her melt-down were no longer there. She said hello to the girls covering the next shift, who looked curiously at her teary face but said nothing. Ethan was standing near the cash waiting for her. As she approached, readying her apology, he stepped forward and hugged her.

"Are you okay?" he asked, letting her go after a few moments.

She nodded. "Look, Ethan," she began, "I'm so sorry …"

"Don't!" he said. "You have nothing to apologize for. Everyone here was cheering you! And don't worry. That is the last time Michael sets foot in this place."

She started to protest, but he cut her off. "I don't want someone that unbalanced working here. Get your things together and go home," he said. "Take as much time as you need. We can cover your shifts if you want a few days off."

"It's okay. I'd rather be working."

"Hey, Ethan!" one of the girls called from the computer section. She was standing in front of the monitors, holding a tray. "I think you better look at this."

"What is it?" Emily asked. Something about her tone made Emily uneasy. Michael had been at that station.

"It's nothing for you to worry about," Ethan said. "Go home."

Ethan patted Emily's arm gently before walking to the computer area.

Emily took off her apron and hung it up with Morgan's in the closet. As they slipped their coats on, getting ready for the walk home, Emily shouted to Ethan, "See you Tuesday at six!"

Ethan didn't respond. He was looking at the monitor and Emily saw he was concerned, more concerned than if it was just a simple computer malfunction.

"What's up, Ethan?" Morgan asked, walking closer.

He looked up at last, seeing her approach. "Just a little problem."

"Can we help?" Emily asked. She wanted to go to him, wanted to see why he was wearing such a concerned expression.

"No, Emily. Thanks. Why don't you just go home? Morgan, could you ask one of the other girls to grab me some out-of-order signs?"

"Sure. How many do you want?"

"All of them."

An uneasy feeling came over Emily. Only a few of the stations were occupied and Ethan was speaking softly to the users, obviously apologizing. She walked closer to the computer area.

"Emily, please don't," Ethan said.

"What is it, Ethan?" What's he done? she asked, her heart growing cold.

"It's nothing you can help with. Listen, you've had a tough day. Just go home and let me handle this."

It was obvious that he was trying to keep her away from the computers. She slipped past him and looked at the first monitor. She saw the café's logo scrolling across, and leaned over the keyboard to nudge the mouse. It took her a moment to understand what she was seeing. Perfectly centred on the screen was a white rectangle that at first glance appeared to be advertising for a lost pet. Then she saw that the photo was of her, one of the ones Michael had used on a card.

The headline read: LOST DOG. Under the picture she read:

BREED: *BITCH*

WILL ANSWER TO NAME: *EMILY TAYLOR*

LAST SEEN: *CHEATING ON BOYFRIEND*

As she watched, the picture started to change, dissolving into a shot of her standing at her bedroom window. Next, it dissolved into another picture, one of her leaning out of a bus, kissing Daniel. This picture didn't fade; instead, it exploded in a mushroom cloud of pixels. Then the sequence started over.

Emily tried to close the file, but the computer was locked. She rushed to the next monitor and saw the same thing. Once more she tried to clear it. She went to each monitor, seeing the same disgusting screen over and over. She couldn't even turn it off because of the grid over each of the computers, to prevent customer tampering.

"Ethan!" she said, nearly crying. "Get rid of them!"

"I can't!" he replied. "He's locked us out somehow."

Morgan was looking at the screens now, swearing loudly.

"That bastard! I swear he's dead next time I see him!"

"Get the main power," Ethan said at last, diving under the desks to pull the power cords from the backs of the computers.

Chapter 13

"I just want you to do something about this person!" Emily's father said.

Emily sat silently as her parents and Ethan discussed the best way to deal with Michael. They sat at a table in the closed-off computer section, as far away from the customers as possible. Her father was normally an easygoing, composed person who rarely raised his voice. Years of teaching teenagers had taught him a lot about patience. It unsettled her to see him being so rude to Ethan. As she listened, she felt herself wavering between feelings of outrage, disgust, and just plain embarrassment about the whole situation. She glanced at the clock and saw it was only a little after three. It was hard to believe all that had happened since noon.

"I'm going to fire him next time he comes in here," Ethan said. He had already explained about not having Michael's correct number.

"I have a better idea." said her father. "Why don't you give me his address so I can go pay him a visit?" Emily smiled and hugged him.

"Oh, Dad," she said. "What are you going to do then? Give him detention?" He smiled and shook his head, running a hand over her back and shoulders.

"It just frustrates me that we can't make this guy leave you alone."

Emily saw her mother was as angry as her husband.

"I can't believe you hired someone without at least checking up on him!"

Ethan started to speak, but Emily interrupted.

"It's not his fault, Mom. I was the one who helped Michael get the job."

"Have you called the police? Can't you have him charged for tampering with your property?"

"I can call our lawyer, but I don't know if what he did is enough reason to have him arrested."

"He's harassing a seventeen-year-old girl. Isn't that enough reason?" her father asked. Emily looked over at the banks of dark monitors. She didn't want to think about how long Michael had been spying on her, taking her picture from a distance. It had been at least long enough to get all those images, all taken at different times over the past six months or so. It was obvious now that he had been following her long before he was hired at the café. And long before the incident with those boys, the one that she had believed had begun this infatuation with her. After what Michael had done today, she had called her parents, asked them to come get her at the café. That was when she told them about how Michael had been bothering her.

"He was at the house today," said her father.

"What?" Emily couldn't believe it.

Her mother nodded. "He was waiting on the front porch swing when your dad and I got home from our walk this morning."

"You didn't let him in, did you?"

Her dad looked annoyed and embarrassed.

"I had no idea who he was. I thought he was just another friend. He seemed to know a lot about us."

"And he was extremely polite, introduced himself as your boyfriend," her mother said.

"You didn't think it was odd that a guy I'm supposedly dating just shows up to introduce himself to my parents?"

They both just shrugged.

"We're going to the school tomorrow, to talk to the principal."

"Do you have to?" Emily asked. She didn't want to be the subject of the student rumour mill yet again. "Can't we just forget all this? I really told him off today. That's why he put those signs on the computer. Maybe he finally got the point."

"Maybe," her father said. "But let's make sure."

* * *

It was a tense ride home from the café. As they walked into the house, Emily brushed past her parents.

"Where are you going?" Her father asked as she walked to the staircase.

"I need a shower, and I just want to be alone for a while."

Her father gestured for her to come back. "We're not through discussing this."

"What else is there to discuss? You've already told me what we're going to do."

Her mother was hanging up her coat.

"That's not fair," she said. "You know we have to let the school know about all of this."

Emily sighed. She just wanted to get this over with, to have her life go back to normal, to never see or hear from Michael ever again.

"You could have told us about this boy long before it came to this," her father added.

"What was there to tell? That some stupid boy has a crush on me?"

"It was more than that, Emily."

"Look," she said. "Let me just have an hour alone, okay? Then we can discuss this all you want."

"Alright," said her mother. She ran upstairs to her room and shut the door. She lay on the bed and closed her eyes, but all she could see was the scene in the café earlier. She still didn't quite believe that it had been her, Emily, acting that way, screaming at Michael. The phone beside her bed rang. She nervously looked over at the call display and felt huge relief to see that it was Daniel calling.

"Hi," she said, grabbing the handset and standing up.

"Where've you been all day?" Daniel asked. "I tried calling and e-mailing you."

She nearly hung up on him. Why was he questioning her? Why did he need to know where she had been? Emily took a moment to relax.

"It's been a strange day," she replied. He must have detected some note in her voice. He hesitated a moment before going on.

"Do you want to tell me about it?"

Emily was walking slowly back and forth between her bed and the computer desk. She hesitated, looking at the silent monitor.

"There's not much to tell. I found out I have a temper today at work."

"What happened? Some lousy customer not tip you again?" Emily could hear the smile in his voice.

She smiled too. "No. It was a bit more serious than that."

"So what happened?"

Emily hesitated again, wondering if she should tell him. She sat down on the edge of the bed.

"Emily? You still there?"

"Still here," she replied. "I was deciding how to tell you this." She paused again. "You see, there's this guy I met at work …"

"Uh, oh," Daniel said, and she heard the chill in his voice. "I think I get where this is going."

It took her a moment to understand what he meant. "No! No, not that!" she laughed. "Oh, God, no! This guy's been harassing me. He's a bit psycho."

"Oh. Well, that's a relief," Daniel said. He laughed, realizing what he had just said. "I mean, you know…"

She smiled and nodded. "It's okay. I know what you meant."

"So what's he been doing?"

She sighed. "It's a bit difficult to tell over the phone."

"Okay. Why don't I come over then?"

Emily was taken aback. "You want to come over? Today?"

"Sure. Why not? It's still early."

She went to her window, pulled open the curtain, and looked outside. Her bedroom window faced the street and she saw that, although the sun was starting to get low in the west, it was still a clear, sunny day. Her first reaction was to say no to his offer. It had been a bad day, and she was pretty certain her parents wouldn't allow Daniel over after what had happened today.

And then she thought how nice it would be to see him, the perfect antidote to the horrible scene at the café. She could at least try to keep her life normal.

"Okay," she said. Then she gave him directions to her place. She hung up the phone and jumped onto her bed, and as she stared at the ceiling, Emily realized she had this big, goofy grin on her face. She knew she'd made the right decision.

Her computer bleeped.

She sat up on the bed and stared at it, fully aware that Michael would send the poster to her home. All she had to do was erase his e-mails without opening them.

Emily stood and leaned over her keyboard, but before she touched it, the screensaver clicked off and she was looking at the computer desktop. She reached down to begin the shut-down procedure, and then jumped back, startled. It was as if someone was sitting at her computer using it. As she watched helplessly, programs launched by themselves. She clicked frantically, trying to close them, but it had no effect. Windows opened and closed and the cursor ran all over the monitor as if possessed.

"Mom! Dad!" she shouted. "Come up here!"

The computer kept operating by itself and she saw the e-mail program on top of the other windows on the desktop. Her parents rushed in.

"Look at this," she said, indicating the monitor. As they huddled around, they watched the cursor scroll down the control buttons for her e-mail.

"Can't you stop it?" her mother asked.

Emily shook her head. "I tried. It's like my keyboard isn't connected. I can't override this."

"Shut it off then!" her father said. He reached under the desk and pushed the power button on the computer. Nothing happened. They stood helpless as the cursor hit the receive button on her e-mail. A barrage of messages flooded in before Emily jumped under her desk and pulled the plug.

"What now?" her mother asked.

"I don't know," Emily said, sitting on the floor, looking up at them.

"Leave it off!" her father said as he ran his hands through his thinning brown hair. She had never seen him so furious.

* * *

It was already dark by the time she and Daniel sat in the sunroom, drinking hot chocolate and staring over the ravine at the mountains. There were no lights in here, so they could easily see outside. High above, there were a few scattered clouds glowing orange from the city lights. They sat close together on the thick cushions of the wicker sofa, neither of them saying a word. It was nice just to be together, and when he casually held her hand, it also felt like the natural thing to do.

It had taken a bit of convincing for her parents to allow him to come over tonight, but they had finally relented. She knew her mother understood how important it was for her to keep her life as normal as possible. Her father was still not happy, even though he was, as always, very polite when she introduced Daniel.

"So. Are you going to tell me about the other guy?"

Emily told him about Michael. It was a quick story, since she couldn't bear to go into every detail. She told him about the blow-up at work, but not the posters that appeared on the computers. That was still too painful to discuss with someone she was just starting to know.

"Why can't some guys just take no for an answer?" Daniel asked, more to himself than her. "And he goes to your school as well?"

"I'm afraid so."

"Are you going to be okay? I mean, if you want, I could meet you at school, make sure he leaves you alone."

She smiled at the offer. "Thanks. But I can handle it. Besides, I have Morgan to take care of me."

"You also have me, now," Daniel slipped his arm over her.

She smiled at him, and leaned against his shoulder. "Thanks."

"No problem."

They sat like that for a while, her head resting on his shoulder, and she could smell his recently shampooed hair, the faint musky odour from his wool sweater. She liked the way he smelled, it was comforting somehow.

"What's that out there?" he asked.

"What?" she replied, a little upset that the

moment was interrupted.

"I keep seeing this light out in the park there."

"Where?" Emily sat up, looking out the windows of the sunroom. There were no streetlights in the park, and it was rare for anyone to be there after dark.

"It's gone now. Probably just someone out looking for their dog."

He pulled her back until she was leaning against his shoulder again. Emily wasn't quite as comfortable as she had been a moment ago. She was wondering about the person out there in the dark.

Chapter 14

They met at the principal's office an hour before classes began. Principal Graham had worked with both of Emily's parents in the past, so they spent the first few minutes catching up, a forced casualness that Emily hated. She just wanted to get this over with. On the way over to the school, she had tried in vain to convince her parents that all of this was pointless. She had tried to tell them that the poster was his last move, a way to get back at her. Even someone as obsessed as he was couldn't keep this fantasy alive after the way she humiliated him in front of all those people.

Principal Graham invited them to sit at the chairs in front of her desk. She sat down and picked up a file that sat on the desk. She patted it as she began to talk.

"After your call last night, I made sure I had a look at Mr. LaVide's file before this meeting."

"Look, Sharon, I know you aren't supposed to discuss students with us …" Emily's mother began.

"There isn't a problem," Graham interrupted. "Michael isn't a student at this school."

"What?" Emily blurted out. "But I've seen him. So have others. People know him here."

"He was a student, but he dropped out last May," she glanced at the file. "Just after his eighteenth birthday."

Graham summarized the file for them, how Michael had been in foster care since he was twelve, and how he had bounced around the system. He had had a difficult time in school and was held back in Grade 7. There was suspicion of some physical abuse at one of the foster homes, but nothing was proven.

Emily thought of the e-mails Michael had sent her, describing his idyllic childhood.

"Apparently, he was doing well at the last foster home. Again, until he turned eighteen. Then he just disappeared. His foster parents own a computer store and he had been working there part-time. After he left, they discovered that someone had entered the store and stolen thousands of dollars worth of equipment."

"Michael?" her father asked.

"That's what we would assume, but his foster parents didn't report him to the police. In fact, they refused to believe he was capable of such a thing."

"Do they know where he's been living?"

"They couldn't say. And you're sure you've seen him on school grounds, Emily?"

"Positive. He's come up to talk to me a few times. And he even gave me one of the gifts at my locker."

As she thought about it, she realized that she had most often spotted him in the halls or outside school. She had never seen him carrying books, never seen him in any classroom.

Principal Graham sat back in her chair, and looked at the file.

"It's bad enough that Michael's been trespassing on school property, pretending to be a student here to be near underage girls. But if he has been actively harassing Emily, that's very serious. I think it might be time to call the police."

Emily cringed. "Do we have to? I mean, can't we just warn him or something?"

"It's gone too far for that, Emily," Principal Graham said. "Much too far."

Chapter 15

The large man standing on her porch introduced himself to her father while Emily and her mother waited in the hall. Two uniformed police officers stood slightly behind him. One was a woman who didn't look much older than Emily. The other was a heavy-set older man with thick-lensed glasses. Both of them held large metal cases.

"I'm Detective Gordon," he said.

Emily's father nodded and shook his hand. "I'm Dave Taylor. Come in. We were expecting you."

The detective walked into the hall and her father introduced him to Emily and her mother.

"I've brought a forensics team to look at your computer. Is that okay?"

Emily nodded at him and at the others. "It's upstairs in my room," she said as she started to climb the stairs. The officers followed.

Upstairs, the older man immediately went to

her computer while the woman checked her entire bedroom carefully. She removed what looked like a pen-sized flashlight from her ceiling fan. The flashlight had a small wire sticking out of one end.

"What is that?" she had blurted out.

The female officer held the object carefully in her latex-covered hands. She looked at Emily and hesitated before speaking.

"It's a camera," she replied gently. Emily covered her mouth with her hands. She wanted to scream. She felt tears sting her eyes.

"A camera!" she said, her voice shaking. "He's been watching me?"

The officer nodded and then placed the camera in a thick plastic bag.

"That son of a bitch!" her father swore. Emily turned to her mother and they hugged. She felt ill.

"I think it would be a good idea to check the rest of the house as well," she said after she placed the bag in a compartment of her metal case. Emily's father just nodded, his face flushed with anger.

Partly from curiosity and partly to keep herself from thinking about what had been found, Emily walked over to the officer working on her computer. He had taken the casing off.

"How did he do that with my computer?"

The older male officer smiled. "Pretty simple, really. You have the latest operating system and it allows you to run your computer remotely. Providing you have the proper access."

"And Michael had that," Emily said. He had all the access he wanted apparently.

"I'm going to make coffee," her mother said. Emily went with her, needing something to do. She and her parents waited downstairs at the kitchen island while the police finished their search. It took less than an hour and then Detective Gordon joined them in the kitchen.

"We didn't find anything else," he said. "But we had to take the computer, to run some tests on it. You should have it back in a few days."

Emily wanted to tell him he could keep it.

She looked at his hands as he reached out and took the mug her mother had offered him. The mug seemed tiny in his hands, and he didn't bother placing his thick fingers in the handle. Her own coffee mug still sat on the island counter untouched. Her hands were still trembling, and she felt her stomach churn with nausea. She had to fight the need to run upstairs and shower, to scrub her skin raw. She felt violated.

"How are you holding up?" the detective asked. He was soft-spoken, which seemed at odds with his physical presence. Emily smiled a bit at the question.

"Okay. I guess," she told him.

Even as early as a few nights ago, she wouldn't have believed she would be sitting in her kitchen talking to a detective about a stalker. It was like something out of a bad movie. She was surprised by how calm she was, considering the fact that she had finally come to understand how crazy Michael really was.

"So what happens now?" Emily asked.

"Right to the point," Gordon said with a slight smile. "Well, do you have a restraining order on Mr LaVide?"

The three of them shook their heads.

"We didn't know we needed one until yesterday," Emily's mother said. "I don't even know how to get one."

"You have to file a statement of claim. Once you do that, you have to appear before a Court of Queen's Bench judge." He smiled, seeing their look of confusion. "Don't worry. I can help you through it."

"I don't know if we have enough proof," her father added. "Until yesterday, the stuff he did was pretty mild."

"With what we found today, we have enough to get a restraining order. And I can start a criminal investigation." Gordon sipped his coffee and turned to Emily again.

"Maybe you should tell me what he's been up to."

Emily explained to him about the e-mails and the cards. She also told him about the incident at work, how he had placed that poster on all the computers.

"Did you keep anything he sent you?" Gordon asked. Emily nodded.

"Most of it."

She stood up from the island, ignoring the looks from her parents and ran up to her room. She glanced quickly at the ceiling fan before reaching under her bed for the shoebox. Back down in the kitchen, her parents and the detective were waiting silently for her as she cleared some room on the island and placed the box on top.

"I threw away his gifts, but I kept the cards he gave me. I also printed out all his e-mails," she said

"Why did you print them?" her father asked, as he reached out to examine some of the printouts.

Emily shrugged and flushed with embarrassment. She couldn't bring herself to admit to them that she had been flattered by Michael's attention at first.

"Proof?" Gordon asked, smiling at her.

"Just being thorough," she said, thankful he gave her a way out of her father's question. Gordon began to take the printouts from the box. Emily had all of them stapled or paper-clipped together in sequence. Some of them were twenty or more pages long. She had used up at least one ink cartridge since all of this had begun.

"Has the tone of the letters changed since yesterday?" Gordon asked.

"In what way?" she asked.

"In cases like this, the letters start off romantically. If the stalker is still rejected, then his behaviour becomes more aggressive. He will start to leave threatening messages, warnings, that kind of thing."

"I haven't looked at … since yesterday. I really don't know if his messages got …"

She explained that they hadn't looked at the computer since it came to life yesterday.

"In any of your encounters with him, has he threatened you or made any comments that would cause concern?"

She shook her head. "He rarely speaks to me in person. Mostly he just stares at me from a distance. The most he's ever said is when he's giving me a present. He seems to be the most comfortable telling me stuff in the e-mails. Yesterday was the first time I saw him really angry with me."

"Do you have any idea what made him angry?"

She sighed and looked at her coffee mug as she answered, running a finger along the rim.

"I went on a date the night before," she told him.

He nodded. "And you think Michael knew that?"

"My mother drove me to the date. I saw Michael on my street, watching."

"Emily!" her mother said. "Why didn't you tell us that?"

Emily couldn't give her an answer. She had just hoped it would all go away.

"Let's start at the beginning," Gordon said, pulling a notebook out of his jacket. "How long have you known Michael LaVide?"

"Maybe three months now. Since he started

working at the café back in September." She told him about the night she had protected Michael from the teenage boys. The detective just nodded once in a while, scribbling in his notebook. Emily felt a little silly thinking about that night. She had thought she was doing the right thing, helping someone, but it had backfired on her. Just like Morgan had predicted.

"I don't mean to embarrass you, but I have to ask. Was there ever any kind of romantic involvement between you?"

"Oh my God, no!" Emily replied. Since she had met him, the idea of dating Michael had gone from ridiculous to repulsive.

"To the best of your knowledge you never did or said anything to give him the idea that you were romantically linked?"

"Never. Ask Morgan! Ask anyone who works with me. They all knew how I felt about Michael. I mean, I was nice to him at the beginning. I kind of felt sorry for him."

"When did the stalking behaviour begin? The gifts, the letters, and so on?"

"It's just so hard to believe," her mother said. "All of this because Emily tried to be nice to the boy."

"It's likely Michael suffers from a disorder called erotomania. He has the delusional belief that Emily loves him. He thinks that he is having an active, reciprocal relationship with her. This type of stalker is pretty rare, and they're usually women."

"Great!" Emily said. "Just my luck."

"The good news for Emily is that this kind of stalker usually doesn't hurt his victim. But those around her can be in danger. The stalker will frequently lash out at people he thinks are keeping him away from his true love: parents, friends, and especially someone he sees as a rival."

Emily felt cold and thought of Daniel. Was he in danger?

"Have you any idea where he might be?" her father asked the detective.

"We'll check his last foster placement. They might have some ideas."

"And then what?" her mother asked. "What happens once you find him?"

"Because of his behaviour, and the items we discovered today, I can apply for what's called a Form Ten, a mental health warrant. With that we can hold him for at least seventy-two hours to determine his mental state. If he is delusional, we then can hold him up to thirty days in a hospital for observation. Even if I can't get the Form Ten, we have plenty of other evidence to hold him with."

"What if something happens and you can't hold him?" her mother asked.

"Then he'll be released until his court appearance."

"That's crazy!"

Gordon nodded. "It's highly unlikely that will

happen. The only thing he has in his favour right now is the fact he has no previous record."

"He has no record?" Emily asked. "I can't be the only girl he's done this to."

The detective looked over at her. "He may have stalked other girls, but no one brought charges. It could also be that his mental health has been slowly getting worse over the years."

"And even if you do hold him the thirty days, what then?" her father asked. "He'll be back on the street ready to come after Emily again?"

"We'll do everything we can to keep him off the street," Gordon said. Her mother shifted uncomfortably in her chair.

"But there's no guarantee, correct?"

Gordon shook his head. "No. There are no guarantees. I'll interview him myself, to get the thirty-day assessment. During that time a doctor will test him to see if he's fit to stand trial or if he should stay in hospital indefinitely for treatment."

"Isn't it better if he goes to jail?" Emily asked.

Gordon shook his head. "It's better he stays in hospital. He could be kept there a long time. If he goes to trial, he probably won't get much jail time. I don't mean to scare you, but that will just put his stalking on hold. I'm pretty sure that once he's released, he'll start again where he left off."

Chapter 16

Emily and the others sat in the café waiting for Daniel's audition. It was a Sunday evening and the place had been closed for about half an hour. Now that it was winter, they closed at six o'clock on Sunday evenings. The only people in the café besides Emily and her parents were Ethan and Joel. Emily thought about the night Morgan had revealed her theory about Ethan and Joel's relationship. Seeing them together, now, Emily could easily see they were more than just business partners. The tiny audience had pulled two tables together in front of the north wall.

Two weeks had passed slowly since the police had arrived at her house. It was the end of November and no one had seen Michael since that afternoon in the café. Ethan had even pinned his final paycheque to the bulletin board with a note written in bright pink marker that read "Here,

Mikey, Mikey!"

Emily tried to keep her life as normal as possible, going to school in the day, keeping her regular shifts at the café in the evenings and on the weekends. This was despite the fact that she was basically grounded otherwise. Her parents made sure she kept very close to home, to keep her safe.

Michael had disappeared and not even the police had been able to track him down so far. The address he had given on his application was as counterfeit as the phone number. It had turned out to be the offices of the Veterinary Society of Alberta. Emily wondered what message Michael was trying to send by using that address.

It had taken five days to get her computer back from the police. They told her to keep checking for e-mails. There was no need for her to keep making copies since they had their own link to her computer, so they could monitor Michael.

Michael did indeed send her e-mails, but they were less frequent. Just as Detective Gordon had predicted, the tone had changed dramatically. Instead of being sweet and sentimental pleas for her affection, these messages were full of hate and threats. The truly weird thing about them was that, even though he now seemed to hate her, their imaginary relationship was apparently going strong and there was no doubt in Michael's mind that they were only going through a rough patch.

Emily was grateful to stop thinking about Michael as she saw Daniel walk down the hall from the rear entrance carrying a guitar. He had his two friends with him, the same ones she had seen weeks before. Rick, the blonde, chubby one, carried a small amp, and Al, the skater boy, carried a microphone. The three of them walked over to the stage, little more than an area cleared away between the tables and the hallway that lead to the back door.

Daniel set up quickly and sat on one of the tall stools provided for him by Ethan. He smiled quickly at the small audience before he tuned his guitar. Emily felt for him — he looked so nervous up there all alone. Satisfied with the guitar, he leaned forward and started to say something into the microphone. He leaned back quickly at a sudden squeal of feedback.

"That isn't part of the act," he said quickly, and the audience laughed at his comment.

Daniel sat up straight on the stool and started to play. After only a few chords of the first song, Emily knew that he was good. Then she looked over at her parents and watched their expressions as Daniel continued to play. He played three tunes, one of them she even recognized — "Mr. Lucky," by John Lee Hooker, one of her father's favourites. At the end of each song, the small audience applauded enthusiastically and Emily felt proud of him. He played three songs before Joel stood.

"I think we've heard enough," Joel said as the applause died down. He stood and walked over to

Daniel, and offered him his hand. Daniel stood up and shook it. Ethan walked over to them and the three of them began speaking quietly together.

"So? What did you think?" Emily asked her parents.

They both nodded, smiling broadly. "Not bad," her father said. "Maybe I can get him to transfer over to my school. We need a good guitar player."

"I think he's going to be busy," Emily replied.

At last the conference was over and Daniel walked over to Emily's table.

"Well?" Emily asked, standing up. "What did they say?"

Daniel smiled, then looked over her shoulder. Emily turned to see her parents standing, eager to hear if he had gotten the gig.

"Well?" Emily said. "What happened?"

He smiled, trying to seem casual.

"Not much," he said, shrugging. "They'll let me play Sunday afternoons."

She yelped and started to hug him, then remembered that her parents were standing right there.

"Sundays! That sucks! I work Sundays."

"So?"

"So? I'd rather just be in the audience."

He grinned at her. "You and Ethan will probably be the audience."

"I'm sorry," she said, realizing she was being selfish. This was his moment. "It's great," she said.

"You did really well tonight," her mother said, touching his arm gently.

Daniel shrugged. "Thanks. If it goes well, they might even pay me."

"I think you have a great future," her father added. He started to ask him questions about his background, why he picked those songs. Emily stopped him. Once her dad started talking music, it was hard to get him to shut up.

They all hung around for a little while longer, finishing their coffees and talking. It was after nine o'clock when they finally started to get ready to leave. Emily's parents offered to give Daniel a lift home — Emily knew it was out of kindness, and also to get a look at what part of town Daniel lived in. He declined, telling them that his friends would drive.

"I guess I'd better pack up the equipment," he said at last.

"I'll help," Emily exclaimed, jumping up. Her father started to get up as well.

"I guess I can help too," he said. Emily's mother put a hand on his arm, stopping him.

"I think they can handle it, Dave," she said. Emily's dad looked at his wife a little puzzled, then seemed to understand. He sat down again.

"I guess they can handle it," he repeated. "We'll wait here."

Emily followed Daniel to the back alley, where the other two were already packing away the equipment.

"So," she said. "I'm dating an official musician. Does that make me a groupie?"

"Officially," Daniel replied.

They stood facing each other, a little awkwardly, not knowing the best way to say goodnight. Finally, he smiled and leaned forward to kiss her. This time she didn't turn away.

* * *

Emily's father parked their old car in front of their gate. The night had turned cold while they were in the café and thick clouds had moved in over the city. As Emily got out of the back of the car, she saw a few flakes of snow start to fall. Her dad held the gate open and waved them ahead.

"Ladies," he said as they walked past him toward the porch. Emily smiled at her dad's cute little habit, then something caught her eye and she looked up at the house. Her mother must have noticed it at the same time she did.

"That's odd," she said. "Didn't we turn the lights off before we left, Dave?"

"I was sure we did," her father replied. Emily was also sure — her parents' routine never varied. Every time they left the house, they would shut off all the lights except the one in the foyer. It was their only concession to the idea someone might break in.

She knew immediately that something was wrong. It wasn't just that the lights were on. Every light in the house was on! As they stood there, the heavy front door opened.

Michael LaVide stepped out onto the porch, grinning pleasantly down at them.

Chapter 17

Emily and her parents stopped dead, looking up at the figure on the porch. Her father swore and started toward him. Emily saw that Michael held something in his hand and grabbed her father's arm.

"Don't go near him, Dad!"

Michael was dressed up, at least for him. Gone was his usual uniform consisting of the army surplus jacket, faded jeans and scuffed sneakers. Instead, he wore a checkered sports jacket, faded brown pants, and dusty black patent-leather shoes. His dirty-blonde hair was slicked down with gel and parted severely on the left side. There was something old-fashioned and out of style about the clothes he wore, and nothing seemed to fit him properly. The white dress shirt he wore was buttoned at the top, but hung loosely around his thin neck. It was as if he had seen the entire outfit on a mannequin at a thrift store and bought it without checking to see if it would fit.

As he walked to the edge of the porch, she saw that all he held in his hands were flowers. It didn't make him any less dangerous.

"Hi, Ems," he said, holding the bouquet out to her as he walked down the steps toward her. "You look beautiful."

Emily looked at him, then back at her parents.

Her father got between his family and Michael.

"What are you doing in our home?" he shouted. Michael only smiled wider, lifting his arm to indicate the door.

"Sorry, Dave. I guess it is late. You know me. Can't wait to see my Ems again. Especially on such a big night."

Emily hated that he had called her that. Only Morgan called her Ems.

"I don't know what you think you're doing, but I want you off my property right now!"

"Are you still worried about what Emily did to me? It's okay. I forgave her. We both know that we were meant to be together. No one can come between us now."

Emily saw that her father was too angry to think clearly. She ran forward and grabbed his arm again, turning him to face her.

"Don't try talking sense with him, Dad. He's crazy. Let's just go over to Morgan's and call the police."

Her father glanced at her briefly, but mostly

kept his gaze on Michael.

"She's right, Dave," her mother said. "Reasoning won't do any good."

He continued to watch Michael, as though he was afraid he would attack at any moment. Then he nodded. He said, "Alright! Go! I'll wait until I see you're safely inside."

"We're not leaving you out here alone," Emily said.

"I'll be fine. Just get to Morgan's."

Emily and her mother started to back up, keeping an eye on Michael.

"Where are you two off to?" Michael called, walking casually down the steps. "We have to start the celebration!"

He started down the walk toward them, but Emily's father put a hand on his chest, stopping him. Her father was at least four inches taller than Michael, and easily outweighed him. It didn't make her feel any better about leaving him alone. Emily and her mother said nothing as they backed out of the yard. At the gate, they spun around and dashed across the street. They ran up the front steps of Morgan's house, and Emily started pounding on the door.

As they waited for a response, Emily looked back at their house. Michael was shouting something, calling to her, and her dad still held him back. She felt a rush of relief as Morgan's parents opened the door, both wearing dressing gowns and looking bewildered. They rushed inside, and

Emily slammed the door shut as her mother hurriedly explained what was happening across the street.

"We have to use your phone to call the police," her mother said. As the adults hurried to the kitchen to use the phone, Emily ran into the living room.

Over the years she had spent almost as much time at this house as she had at her own. Without asking, she opened the drapes to look across the street. She saw her dad still standing on the walk and Michael seemed to be yelling, his arms waving wildly. The bouquet of flowers was lying on the grass.

Morgan walked down the stairs only half-awake, her dressing gown hung loosely over her shoulders.

"What's all the racket?" she said, yawning. Then she saw Emily looking out the front window and came fully awake.

"Ems? What's going on?"

"It's Michael," Emily said. "He's at my house."

Morgan rushed over to join her and as she did, the front door opened and Emily's father rushed inside. The other adults were coming back down the hall from the kitchen.

"What's going on?" her mother said, rushing over to him.

"He started screaming at me, all this trash about keeping Emily and him apart. About how it was all some conspiracy. Then he locked himself inside. He's inside our house!"

"The police are on their way." Her mother told him.

Her father nodded and his wife ran into his arms. He hugged her, and then Emily walked over to join them. He put his arm around her as well and she buried her head in his chest and started to cry.

"I'm so sorry," she said. "It's all my fault."

"None of this is your fault," her father said, holding her tighter. "Don't ever think that."

It took only a few minutes for the first police car to pull up outside their house, lights flashing brightly in the cold evening. Her father ran out as soon as the officers stepped out of the cruiser. The rest of them stayed inside to watch from the warmth and safety of Morgan's house.

There were more flashing lights as an EMS pulled up and parked next to the cruiser. Paramedics rushed out and opened the rear doors to pull out a stretcher. Its thin, wheeled legs sprang into place under it as they lifted it from the vehicle. Emily looked past them toward her home. She could see the living room windows, saw the shadow of someone rushing back and forth against the drawn curtains.

Then she heard shouting from inside her house, the sound of glass shattering and of something heavy falling. Her mother held her hands to her face, trying to hide her tears. The police officers ran up to the front porch. Shocked, Emily saw them draw their guns before they rushed inside.

Emily and her mother came out to the street to stand with her father. Morgan followed, still only wearing her bathrobe over her flannel pyjamas. Snow fell heavily now, and the night had turned much colder.

"Emily!" a voice shouted. They all looked up and saw Michael at a window above the porch, her parents' bedroom window. He pulled back the blinds and must have spotted Emily standing in the street.

"Emily! It's okay now," he shouted. "I'm here to take you away from them!"

"Michael!" she shouted back. "Just come out!"

"No! Not until they let you go. You have to get away from them! Run, Emily, run now!" He was screaming at her, and even from this distance she could see the wild look in his eyes.

Then, he pushed up the window and kicked out the screen, jumping out onto the roof of the porch. "I'll create a diversion, Emily. Just run, now! Get away to our spot. To the safe house I told you about!"

She had no idea what he meant.

As he yelled down to her, Michael moved closer and closer to the edge of the roof. He was only inches away from the branches of a pine tree at the corner of their home. The porch roof was no more than fifteen feet high, but it was high enough for him to hurt himself. The two officers appeared at the window and she heard them shout at him, ordering him to lie down.

He ignored them

As Emily watched, Michael kept pacing back and forth.

"Why are you still there, Ems! Go while you can. Please. They'll never let us be together!"

"Just leave me alone!" she shouted.

He stopped and stood perfectly still, and it looked as though he was staring at her. Then he tilted his head back to look up at the sky. Emily looked up as well, wondering what he was looking at. Michael held his hands up to the sky, as if trying to catch the flakes of snow that fell to earth.

"Look, Ems," he said, laughing, "it's the final sign. The one I told you about."

As he spoke, he walked forward, not paying attention to his footing.

"Michael!" Emily called out as he stepped closer and closer to the edge.

"Look, Ems," he said, "the stars!" He laughed as he tilted his head back up. "The stars are crashing down!"

At that moment, he reached the edge of the roof and slipped off, tumbling into the branches of pine, twisting as he fell. He landed face first into the bare shrubs planted around the sides of the porch. Emily didn't think he had even tried to break his fall.

Michael lay motionless while the two police officers ran back downstairs. One knelt over him while his partner yelled for the paramedics.

Emily stood shivering in the evening chill as the snow began falling more heavily, the wet flakes landing on the blanket covering Michael as they wheeled him into the back of the waiting EMS vehicle. Her parents hugged her as they watched it race away northward.

* * *

While the police inspected their home, Emily and her parents sat in Morgan's kitchen drinking tea. There had been some attempt at conversation, but after a while no one tried anymore.

After an hour, Morgan's father excused himself and went to bed, explaining he had to get up early for work the next day.

Morgan's mother struggled to keep her eyes open until Emily's mother finally persuaded her to go to bed too.

"It's okay, Sharon," she said. "You don't have to sit up with us. Go to bed."

"I can't just leave you here," she replied. "Maybe I could set up the spare bedroom for you."

"Don't worry," Emily's father replied. "They must be almost finished. You go to bed."

She nodded and said goodnight. Morgan offered to stay up, but she was also nodding off. Emily told her to get some sleep.

"I'm not going to let some lunatic keep me from my own house," Emily's mother said when they were alone.

It was another hour before the police finally allowed them back inside the house. Both she and her mother burst into tears when they walked in and saw the devastation Michael had caused. He had toppled the shelves in the living room, thrown books and records into the fireplace, including her parent's precious collection of vinyl records. The furniture was overturned, throw cushions and their Navajo rug were tossed into the corners. The heavy oak coffee table sat in pieces on top of her parents' overturned sofa.

In the kitchen he had pulled every item he could find from the pantry and the cupboards, and canisters filled with sugar and flour had been smashed against the wall. Michael had found the small shelf that held her parents' wine and had smashed the bottles on the tiled kitchen floor. Emily's father just held his wife as she cried, seeing room after room filled with mindless destruction.

"Why?" she said over and over again. "Why would he do this to us?"

Emily couldn't watch their pain any longer and made her way upstairs. The staircase was littered with more books, sheets, and pillows, as well as the lamps and end tables from her parents' bedroom.

She opened the door to her own room and was amazed to find it untouched. She entered warily, afraid that Michael had left some trap for her.

Emily looked around and saw nothing, and she wondered if perhaps he hadn't come in here. She walked around the room and it seemed that nothing was out of place. Lastly, she opened her closet door and looked inside. At first glance, it also appeared untouched. Then, on the bottom right corner, she saw something that hadn't been there before. It was a shoebox. Emily knelt down to examine it more closely. It seemed innocent enough, but to be safe, she walked over to her desk and took a small plastic ruler from a drawer. Using the tip of the ruler, she lifted the lid of the shoebox very, very warily and let it slide off onto the floor. Then she used the ruler to drag the box out of the closet. She leaned over the box to look inside. She saw a pair of shoes, covered by what appeared to be white satin. The shoes were sitting on a matching satin pillow. Wedding shoes, Emily thought.

This was something the police had missed in their search of the house, obviously in the belief it belonged here. She knew that she shouldn't touch it, but she was curious as well.

Still being careful, she lifted the shoes and the pillow together and placed them on top of her bed. There was something folded in the bottom of the box. She used the ruler again to lift it out. Unfolding it, she saw that it was pages torn from some pornographic magazine. They weren't just typical porn, instead, the images showed women in a series of humiliating, degrading positions. Her first impulse was to flush the pages down the toilet, but she stopped. She knew they were evidence now. Emily turned back to the shoes and saw that the left one was filled with uncooked rice. Prodding it with the ruler she spotted a few quarters and nickels mixed up with the rice. In the right shoe was salt — after prodding it with the ruler, she found a few tiny baby figurines, moulded from pink plastic. There were five figures in all, none more than an inch long. She lifted each shoe carefully to look underneath at the sole. On the heel of the left shoe, Michael had used a black marker to scrawl the word PROSPERITY. On the heel of the right he had written FRUITFULNESS.

Carefully, she placed the little tableau back in the shoebox and laid it on her desk. She would show it to her parents in the morning. They had seen enough for one night.

Downstairs, she heard the vacuum cleaner and knew her parents had begun to clean up the mess. She closed her bedroom door and walked back downstairs, clearing away the items littering them as she went. Emily saw her mother was working in the kitchen, sweeping the debris off the island and the counters onto the floor. Her father was vacuuming the living room rugs, having piled whatever he could salvage from the mess on top of the sofa. Emily watched her mother for a few moments.

"I'm so sorry, Mom," she said, feeling the tears come again.

Her mother put down the broom and held her. "None of this is your fault."

"But our house," Emily said. "Look what he's done to it!"

Her mother shook her head. "It's only things. That's all he could destroy."

It took them until three in the morning to make the place look somewhat decent. Michael had smashed nearly everything breakable in the living room, including their framed family pictures and the antique mirror over the piano, an heirloom from Emily's grandmother. After tossing her parents' carefully arranged music collection into the fireplace, he had obviously tried to burn them. Luckily, he hadn't opened the flue and the fire hadn't caught. All they found in the grate were some ashes and scorch marks on the covers. As they cleaned, she saw her mother sigh each time she found yet another precious item destroyed by Michael's insane rage.

"Why don't you go to bed, honey?" her father said. He looked as tired as she felt. "We can finish this in the morning."

Emily nodded, too tired to argue, and walked up to her room again. She was looking forward to falling into bed, hoping she would be able to sleep. During the hours of cleaning, she had forgotten about the condition of her room. It may have escaped his anger, but he had still been in here.

Furiously she ran over to her bed, ripping the

blankets and sheets from it. She pulled the cases off her pillows and threw them in a pile on the floor. She emptied her closet of clothes, pulled drawers from her dresser and emptied their contents onto the growing pile on the floor. Then she gathered it all up in the quilt and staggered down to the laundry room, stuffing as much as she could into the washer. She grabbed cleaning supplies — detergents, rags and sponges — and ran back up to her room. Emily cleaned every surface he might have touched. She washed the windows and the wooden frames, scrubbed her night table and her desk. She took a fresh toothbrush from the washroom and cleaned between every key of her computer keyboard. When she was finished, she sat heavily on her clean desk chair and looked over the room, exhausted. With the last of her strength, she grabbed a blanket from the linen closet and walked down the hall to the spare room her parents had turned into an office. There was an old leather couch against the far wall and she lay down on it. She was exhausted, but she found she couldn't bring herself to sleep in her own room.

It took a while, but she finally slept.

Chapter 18

Morgan came over after supper the next day and they went up to Emily's bedroom. Emily had stayed home, not ready to face everyone. The little incident had made the evening news and was the main subject of conversation at school. Morgan promised to slap around anyone who said anything bad about her friend.

"Have you talked to Daniel yet?" Morgan asked.

Emily nodded. He had called after school.

"Why isn't he here?"

"He offered, but I told him it was probably better if he left it for a couple of days."

"Why?"

Emily shook her head. "I don't know. It just feels weird to be with a guy right now. Any guy. I need time to figure out how I feel about all this."

"Why?"

Emily felt herself getting angry at Morgan's

endless questions. It seemed she was angry most of the time these days.

"Look, I can't explain it! I just want to be alone, okay?"

Morgan leaned back, startled by Emily's outburst. There was an awkward silence, broken by the sound of the telephone ringing. Emily let her parents answer.

"Look, I know you're upset, but don't take it out on me. Or Daniel. After something like this, he probably wants to be there for you. We all do."

"I know," Emily said. "I'm sorry. I just need to work through it. I'll call Daniel when I'm ready."

"Just don't wait too long," Morgan said.

As she said this, there was a soft knock on her bedroom door. Her father opened the door slowly. Emily couldn't tell what he wanted from his blank expression. He still looked tired from too little sleep.

"That was Detective Gordon," he said.

"What happened" she asked.

"He wanted to let you know that the court order went through. Michael will be held for a thirty-day assessment."

"That's great," Emily said, trying to sound happier than she felt. "Thanks, Dad."

When he closed the door again, Emily just rubbed her eyes wearily.

"What's with the look?" Morgan asked. "You should be happy he's been put away!"

Emily shook her head. "It's only for thirty days. What happens after that?"

Chapter 19

The telephone rang.

Emily was at her desk, doing homework. She stood and walked over to her nightstand and checked the call display on her phone. For a moment, she thought about letting it ring.

She took a deep breath and lifted the handset.

"How have you been?" Daniel asked.

"Okay. How are you?"

"Okay," he replied

There was a slight pause on the other end.

"I know you asked me to wait to call, but I just wanted to make sure you're okay."

"I'm fine," she replied.

"You don't sound it," he said.

"I am, really," she lied. "Look, I'm just in the middle of some homework, so maybe …"

"What did I do wrong?" he said quickly, interrupting her.

"What?"

"You heard me. What did I do to get you so pissed at me?"

Emily sat on her bed, and saw that her hands were shaking.

"I'm not mad at you," she said at last, trying to get her emotions under control.

"Come on, Emily! It's been what, almost a week since they arrested that guy? And you've avoided me totally!"

"I can't believe you're acting like this!" she replied. "I haven't wanted to talk to anyone! So what makes you think you're so special?"

As soon as she spoke the words, she regretted them. It was something she had done a lot lately, reacting angrily to the smallest of annoyances.

There was another long pause.

"You're right. I guess it was stupid of me to think I was special to you," he said.

"Wait!" she said gently. "I didn't mean it like that! I'm sorry."

She felt her eyes start to well up as she sat on the bed, rocking back and forth.

"I just need time. It's not you, really. It's me." She said. "I just need some time alone."

She heard a sigh on the other end and waited for him to respond.

"Sure," he said at last. "Remember that time on the phone, the first time you told me about this guy?"

"I guess," she said, trying to remember the conversation.

"You said something like, 'Daniel, we have to talk. I met this guy at work.'"

She smiled. "I remember."

"I thought you were dumping me because of him."

He paused again and she waited, feeling her heart pound, knowing what was coming and powerless to change it.

"I guess I was right."

Chapter 20

Emily glanced at the calendar on the wall where she kept track of her shifts at the café. She had only worked a few shifts over the last two weeks, and tonight was her first night working with Morgan in a week. On the same calendar she had carefully marked Michael's release date, December 24, only ten days away now.

Her parents were at their usual spot at the kitchen island, drinking coffee and marking papers when the doorbell rang.

"That's Morgan," Emily said, heading to the door. They had planned to walk together to work. It was already dark outside, but a chinook was blowing, making it a perfect night for walking.

"The offer's still good," her father shouted. "I can drive you."

"We'll be fine. Besides, I've been cooped up so much I need the exercise."

She opened the heavy wood door and looked up, startled. Detective Gordon stood on the porch.

"Hi, Emily," he said. "Can I come in?"

She saw the look on his face and knew that he hadn't come all the way here to give her good news.

"Sure," she said, stepping aside to let him in.

"Are your folks here? I need to talk to them as well."

"Is everything okay?" Emily asked, his dour look telling her it wasn't. She heard footsteps and turned to see her mother walking down the hall.

"Detective," she said, looking as nervous as Emily felt. "What's the matter?"

Emily wondered if this was the way life went for cops. No one was happy to see you show up at the door.

"I just wanted to keep you up to date on Michael's status."

"His status?" Emily asked. "He's in hospital."

"We were just having coffee," her mother said. "Why don't you come back to the kitchen and join us?" Now Emily's father had joined them. The four of them stood in the tight hallway, looking at each other uncomfortably.

"Thanks for the offer, but this won't take long," Gordon said. He looked at Emily before continuing. "Michael's been given an early release so he can spend Christmas with his foster family."

"He's what?" Emily shouted. All of them spoke at once, wanting to know what was going on.

Detective Gordon held up his hands, pleading with them to calm down. When they stopped, he explained.

"It seems that, technically, he's still under their care. They've been visiting him often and are convinced that he's doing well. They think he's a victim as well. That he's just a kid who had a crush on a girl and acted stupidly."

"These are the same people who didn't report him when he stole thousands of dollars in equipment from them, right?" Emily's father asked.

"They are."

"I thought that Michael had to stay locked up," Emily asked, angry now. "That it was a court order!"

Gordon nodded, looking just as frustrated. "Michael is a very intelligent guy. Most stalkers are. He's been an exemplary patient, telling the doctors exactly what they want to hear. He's keeping the right balance of regret for his actions and not being fully aware of what he did."

"So when is he going to be released?"

"This weekend. But …!" he added when they all started yelling again. "His foster parents have arranged to take him to Mexico over the holidays. When he gets back, he has to surrender himself back to the hospital to continue the assessment."

"Wonderful! So now he gets a tropical vacation instead of being locked up?" her mother said. She shook her head, too angry to continue.

"The foster parents have signed a statement

taking full responsibility for him. He isn't to be allowed out without their supervision. And don't worry. I'll be keeping a close eye on all of them."

Her father rubbed the back of his neck, looking like he couldn't believe any of this was really happening.

"What's with these people?" he asked. "Don't they see how sick this kid is?"

No one had an answer for him. Emily had a new thought.

"Remember when Michael disappeared for days after what he did to the computers?" The others nodded. "His foster parents said they had no idea where he was. I bet they knew exactly where he was. I bet they were hiding him."

"It's a bit of a stretch, Emily," her mother replied, then looked at Gordon. The detective did not seem surprised by the idea.

"It's something I looked into. I just can't prove it."

He put a hand on Emily's shoulder, and apologized one more time before saying goodbye.

"I better go get Morgan," Emily said, dazed by what had just happened.

"You're not still going to work?" her father asked.

"It's better than sitting here all night thinking about how lousy this is."

Chapter 21

It was early on Sunday morning when her parents dropped her at the front door to begin her first full day shift. They weren't happy about leaving her, particularly since Michael had been released on Friday. Emily was a little nervous herself, but she knew that the police were watching him, and that he was scheduled to take a plane to Mexico that afternoon.

"Are you sure you're okay?" her mother asked one more time.

"I'm sure," Emily replied.

"And you've got your phone?"

Emily took her brand new cellphone out of her coat jacket. For years her parents had been adamant about her not having a cellphone while she lived under their roof. They had seen the way the phones had come to dominate teenage life. But the night Detective Gordon had arrived to tell them about Michael's release they ran out to a mall and bought her the phone. One of the first people they had given the number to was Detective Gordon.

"It's right here, Mom," Emily replied. "All charged up and ready for action."

She waved at them as she walked up to the café's doors.

Christmas was less than a week away and she was already sick of hearing carols. To make things worse, Ethan had dusted off his antique collection of cheesy Christmas CDs, playing them over and over. As she walked in the door, the first thing she did was look to her right, toward the back of the café and the computer stations. It had become a habit she couldn't seem to shake. Particularly today.

"Emily!" Ethan called out as he came out of the storage room and spotted her. He walked over to her, arms outstretched, and gave her a hug. It felt good. Over the last few weeks Ethan had become more than just a boss.

"I can't believe you came in today! I would be holed up in a hotel someplace!"

She had told him about Michael's release on her last shift.

"Life goes on, right?" she said, trying to sound braver than she felt.

He led her back to the counter and sat her down like she was a special customer. Ever since the whole Michael debacle had begun, he had apologized to her over and over for not acting sooner to get rid of him. She had explained to him that the obsession had begun long before Michael had started to work at the café.

Ethan poured her a mug of her favourite blend.

"Here's to locking him up and throwing away the key," Ethan said, raising his own mug for a toast. They tapped their mugs together.

"Let's hope," Emily said.

"Now tell me, what's going on with Daniel and you?"

She looked at him. "Nothing. Why?" Emily didn't really want to have this conversation. She put her mug on the counter and walked to the storage room to get her apron.

"He called me yesterday wanting to cancel the performance this afternoon."

"He did? Why?"

Ethan filled his coffee cup. "Because of you. I guess you must have had a falling out?"

"You could call it that." She slipped the apron over her head, tying it up as she continued. "You did tell him he should play, right?"

"Of course! I've even marked it on the board."

Emily looked out the window at the sandwich board. On the chalk part, under some badly drawn holly leaves, Ethan had written:

"Today's Special: A Seasonal Selection of Music Performed Live!"

"Seasonal?" Emily asked. "Daniel plays the Blues."

Ethan shrugged. "So he can sing Blue Christmas!"

Emily nodded, feeling a little weird about seeing Daniel. She had missed him, of course, but still wasn't ready to date. She glanced at the board again, seeing Daniel's name there. She was glad he was still playing. She didn't want her crazy life to mess him up.

* * *

Emily glanced up at the clock and saw that it was getting close to one o'clock, Daniel's scheduled time. She was in the rear of the café, taking an order and listening to one of the customers complain that his computer was acting up (the new person who fixed them now wasn't as readily available as Michael had been). She looked up and saw Daniel and his friend arrive. Emily walked back to the counter to fill her orders, making sure she made no eye contact with them. As he set up, she tried to appear as busy as possible.

Daniel took his time setting up, and she wondered if he was trying to avoid her as well. It took about twenty minutes before he approached her. Emily sat behind the counter with Morgan, keeping her back to the stage area.

"Hi," he said, smiling at her.

"Hi," she replied.

"We're in the middle of something," Morgan told Daniel. Emily knew she was trying to save her some embarrassment.

"It's okay, Morgan," Emily told her. She patted her friend's arm.

"Can I talk to you?" he asked. She stood up and slipped past Morgan.

"Come here a minute," Emily said, and Daniel followed her. She sat at the counter along the windows. Instead of sitting with her, he just stood, waiting for her to speak. She'd had weeks to prepare for this and still wasn't sure how she felt at actually seeing him again.

"Look," she said. "What do you want to happen? Between you and me, I mean."

Daniel shrugged. "I want to keep seeing you, I guess."

"You guess?" she said, smiling.

"You know what I mean. I want to see you. I miss you."

She nodded. It had been easy telling herself that she didn't care about him when he wasn't standing right in front of her. It was an overwhelming feeling, as though somehow the way she acted right now would affect her life from that moment on. It seemed she had two choices. Choose the boy and go back to being a normal, teenage girl. Or, say goodbye to him and look over her shoulder forever.

And then the moment passed and she knew that the choice had been made months ago when a disturbed boy chose her. She knew that Michael would never stop, and she knew that anyone close to her would be in danger.

Emily glanced at her watch. "It's time for you to go on," she said.

"Is that it?" he asked.

Emily stood, gave him a gentle kiss on the cheek and walked back behind the counter. Opening the storage room door, she reached inside and grabbed her coat. She slipped past Morgan as she put the coat on.

"Emily," Morgan said, "where are you going?"

"Outside," she replied.

"Don't you want to hear Daniel?"

"I'll hold the door open to hear. I just need to get some air."

She walked down the hall and pushed the steel bar to open the door. Emily hesitated, hearing Ethan introducing Daniel. At the other end of the hall she heard quiet applause, and then Daniel started to play his guitar.

The chinook had blown itself out and it had turned cold outside. A few flakes of snow were visible in the weak winter light. The cinder block they used to prop the door open was buried under some fresh snow. Emily didn't need it, she leaned against the door, looking up at the sky, listening to the sound of Daniel's guitar.

Emily heard a thin, metallic chirp.

She looked around, wondering where the sound came from. She heard it again and realized it was coming from her coat pocket. Feeling stupid at not recognizing the sound of her own phone, she pulled it out of her pocket and looked at the read-out. She immediately flipped the phone open.

"Hello?"

"Emily?" Gordon's voice sounded brittle and distant.

"Hi," she said. "What's going on?" She assumed that he was giving her a report on Michael. He had promised her that he would personally watch him get on the airplane.

"Listen to …" the signal broke up and she heard a crackle of static. Emily shifted around, trying to get the signal back. Finally, she walked further into the alley, trying to get a better connection.

"Detective Gordon? Hello?" she shouted into the phone.

"… lost him at the airport," she heard him say. "He slipped past the crowd at the boarding gate."

"Michael?" Emily shouted. "You lost him?"

She was having difficulty comprehending what he meant. How could he lose him? He was on a plane!

"Your parents told me you're at work. I'm on my way and I've dispatched a cruiser."

More static.

"… stay inside, Emily. Keep plenty of people around you until the car gets there. Understand?"

"Yes," she said, terrified. She closed the phone and slipped it back in her pocket, and walked to the door.

The door had slowly swung closed when she

had walked away from it. Emily hadn't heard the click.

"No!" she screamed and ran to the door, pulling at the handle. It didn't budge. She pounded on it, hoping someone would hear her. She put her ear against the cold metal of the door, listening. Daniel was still playing, drowning out any noise she made.

Thinking quickly, she took out her cellphone and dialed the café's number. It took six rings before someone picked up.

"Afternoon, Cyber Taste Café," Morgan said. Emily could barely hear her over the sound of guitar music.

"Morgan!" Emily screamed into the phone. "It's me! I'm locked out!"

"Hello?" Morgan replied. "I can't hear —"

"Morgan!" Emily screamed again. "Open the back —"

"Can you call again in about half an hour?" Morgan said, interrupting her. Then the line went dead. She felt like throwing the phone as hard as she could against the brick wall of the building. Instead, she shoved it back in her pocket and looked around. The café was almost directly in the centre of a row of buildings taking up the entire block. She began to run to her left, heading east, the shortest way back onto Ninth Avenue.

She felt snow and tears on her cheeks as she ran frantically down the alley, slipping in the soft-packed snow, splashing through icy puddles in her canvas trainers. At the corner she slipped again, and barely avoided sliding under the wheels of a taxi turning into the alley.

The driver hit his horn, and she heard him yelling as she kept running.

Emily turned right, and ran through the used car lot on Twenty-third Street, then right again down Ninth to the café. As usual, the street was busy with traffic, but there were no pedestrians on the sidewalk. The sudden change in weather was probably keeping them indoors.

Emily ran past the antique shop, past the Irish pub, its outdoor terrace closed for the season. Then, just as she passed the pub, the doors of the café sprang open and people began rushing out. Emily ran faster, trying to keep her footing on the ice-and-snow-covered sidewalk. She spotted Morgan and Ethan near the doors, staring inside, looking terrified.

"Morgan!" Emily screamed as she approached, pushing her way through the customers who still stood nearby. In the distance, she heard the wail of a police siren.

"Emily!" Morgan shouted and ran toward her, grabbing her in her arms. "I thought you were inside with him!"

Emily didn't have to ask who Morgan meant.

She slipped past Morgan and looked inside the café windows. Michael was in the centre of the room walking back and forth and yelling at someone. As she looked closer, her face only inches from the glass, she saw who he was screaming at.

Daniel sat on the makeshift stage, his back pressed against the brick rear wall. He looked terrified.

"No!" she screamed and started to pull the doors open. She pulled as hard as she could but they wouldn't move. Ethan and Morgan pulled her back.

"He locked them," Ethan told her.

"Give me the keys!" she shouted. Ethan shook his head.

"They're inside," Ethan said. "Michael's got some kind of device. He showed up out of nowhere and threatened to firebomb the place if we didn't get out."

"All of us except Daniel," Morgan said. "He wouldn't let him leave."

Emily saw that he held what looked like a small thermos container. She also saw that he was wearing a thin raincoat over a brightly coloured shirt and cargo-style shorts. Dressed for his tropical vacation, Emily thought.

Neither Morgan nor Ethan were wearing coats, and they held their arms tight against their body, shivering in the frigid weather.

Daniel was only a few feet from the hallway and the rear door. She found herself trying to will him to his feet, to make a run for the exit.

"Why doesn't he run?" Emily said.

"He wouldn't make it in time," Ethan replied.

"Emily!" Michael shouted as he moved closer to the door. He kept turning his head to make sure Daniel stayed where he was.

"The police are on their way," Emily shouted through the glass of the doors.

Michael laughed, "That's great!" he said. "I remember. Just like that night with those boys. The way you scared them off."

"I'm serious, Michael."

"And what am I?" he screamed, his smile gone, replaced by a wild, frightening anger. "When have I ever been anything but serious when it came to us?"

Emily leaned back a little from the door, her heart pounding even faster.

"What do you want?" she asked.

"It's time to choose," Michael said. He waved the small thermos toward Daniel and then brought it back, lifting it and holding it toward his chest. He tilted his head slightly, waiting for her reply.

She shook her head, tears mixed with snow on her lashes and cheeks and she brushed them away, blinking.

"Don't do this, Michael, please."

He said nothing, just repeated the movement, swinging the thermos at Daniel, pressing it up against his chest again. Emily reached down to the handles and pulled at them, screaming in rage as they refused to budge once more.

"I can't do this, Michael," she screamed through the door. "Please don't make me!"

He walked closer to the door and leaned down until their faces were only inches apart, separated by the glass.

"I'm not the bad guy here, Ems," he said calmly. "You knew what we had together, and it wasn't enough."

"Shut up, you freak!" she screamed. As she looked at him, she saw a movement behind him. Daniel was creeping slowly away from the stage, his back against the brick wall, heading for the exit. Michael must have noticed that she wasn't looking at him.

He straightened up and spun around, seeing Daniel scrambling off the stage and starting to run.

"Run, Daniel!" Emily screamed. "Run!"

Michael stopped and looked at her, and she saw the hurt in his eyes.

"You made your choice," he said.

He turned away, pulling the lid from the thermos, and as he ran after Daniel, he threw it. The thermos crashed against the brick of the wall next to the hall. It fell to the stage, landing beside the amplifier. Nothing happened for one brief moment, and then she caught a glimpse of a liquid spilling out before the entire stage exploded into flame.

She covered her eyes, amazed by the suddenness of the flame, the intensity. She could smell the smoke mix with a heavy, chemical odour. Emily remembered the odour. It was the same as the one in the air all those weeks before, the day Justin's car had exploded in the parking lot at school.

Behind the stage were posters and potted silk plants, all of them feeding the flames. Exposed wooden beams caught next, carrying the fire across the café in every direction. Through the smoke and flames she saw Michael standing perfectly still, looking up at the destruction as if even he was surprised at how fast it had happened.

Then, through the smoke, she saw a flash of daylight at the other end of the hall and knew that Daniel had made it to the exit. Emily felt ecstatic, believing he was out.

The fire licking against the ceiling of the hallway exploded once more into a rolling mass of blue flames, feeding off the sudden influx of air from the open door. And as Emily watched, the sudden change in air pressure slammed the door shut again, and she had no way of knowing for certain if Daniel had made it outside.

All of it had happened in the space of only a few seconds.

Michael looked at her, his face blackened by the smoke. Then he sank to his knees before toppling to the tiled floor. The smoke from the hallway rolled over him and he disappeared from her sight.

Emily looked around, trying to think of something to use to break the windows. Then she spotted the heavy wooden sandwich board on the sidewalk.

"Help me!" she shouted, running to the sign trying to lift it up. Ethan and Morgan ran to her. Together, the three of them lifted the sign and ran toward the café window. They rammed the window as hard as they could, but the sign bounced off. More people started to appear out of nowhere, drawn by the fire and the sound of the alarms inside the building.

"Again!" she shouted. Once more, they ran at the window, and this time the wooden sign left a crack.

"Give it to us," a man shouted. He stood with two other men, all of them easily outweighing Emily and the others. They let go of the sign and the men grabbed it, ramming the window once again. At last it broke through, and one of the men tripped, falling into the broken window as shards of glass rained down — miraculously, none of them hit him. He scrambled to his feet, wrapping his scarf over his mouth and ran inside. Moments later he reappeared, dragging Michael to the window. The others rushed to him, lifting Michael over the window frame and the exposed and jagged glass.

Emily went to the shattered window and the sign lying in the frame and tried to rush inside. The men grabbed her and dragged her back from the burning building.

"Daniel!" she screamed. "We have to get him."

The men who held her said nothing, just looked at the wall of smoke billowing from the café. She heard sirens and turned to see a police cruiser pull up, followed almost immediately by fire engines.

Emily broke free and ran, retracing her path

back down Ninth Avenue, hearing Ethan and Morgan yelling behind her. At the alley she turned west and kept running, slipping and falling on the ice, forcing herself to her feet again to keep running.

She ran past a dumpster and some parked cars and saw a figure lying on his back in the snow beside the picnic table. Emily crouched down beside Daniel, and touched his cheek. His eyes were shut, and she saw soot had covered them and left little smudges under his nostrils. The falling snow melted on his warm skin and she used it to wipe the soot from his face. As she did, he opened his eyes and looked up at her. He lifted a hand toward her and she held it gently by the fingers, careful not to touch the blistered flesh on his palm.

Emily lifted him up and cradled his head against her chest, rocking him back and forth, not letting him go until the paramedics arrived to treat him.

Chapter 22

Emily sat at her favourite chair in her favourite café.

She sipped her espresso and looked out at the crystal blue water of the harbour. Fishing boats were docked for the afternoon, and she watched them as they bounced hypnotically on the waves. The fishermen joked as they prepared their nets for the next day's outing. She could only understand bits and pieces of their conversation, but her language skills were improving each day. A gigantic blue-and-white oceanliner sailed by, heading for the open sea, and she could see the jagged coast of the nearby islands slowly come back into view behind it.

It was late afternoon and most of the locals had gone home for siesta. This late in the season her café was one of the few catering to the tourists who still hung about. An American couple sat a few tables over from her, talking loudly, oblivious to the silence in the small village. A teenage couple sped past on a moped, laughing. Emily looked at her watch and saw it was nearly time to prepare her lessons for the afternoon.

Emily finished her coffee and stood, leaving enough money to pay for the bill and a generous tip. She always tipped coffee shop waitresses well. She grabbed her notes and her books and slipped them into the carrying case that held her laptop computer. The laptop had been a going-away gift from her parents and had the latest wireless connections so that she could e-mail them from anywhere. After what had happened last December, she had needed to take some time off, to get away for a while. She had left school as soon as she could, her parents pulling a few strings at the school board. It was fortunate that she had always been a good student. They had arranged for her to take part in a student exchange program.

"Where do you want to go?" they had asked.

"Any place far from here," she had replied. Her only other stipulation was that it would be remote, hard to find. So now here she was, being warmed by the Mediterranean sun.

She walked down the cobbled streets, past the cathedral and its ornate fountain where small children played with a nearly deflated soccer ball. Ahead of her was a steep hill that led to the narrow alleys and whitewashed buildings. The house that her sponsor family owned was on the far end of the alley. They were both teachers, like her parents, and they had been kind to her, as well as mindful of her need for privacy. Her life here was dramatically different than the one in Calgary, the rhythms of her day now dictated by the heat of the sun and the rise and fall of the tide. Life here had not changed much for centuries.

She had nightmares nearly every night in which she saw Michael's face, grinning at her, lit in an orange glow. And in her nightmares she cradled Daniel's head in her lap as snow and fire billowed around them, blasting the flesh from his bones.

Both boys had recovered of course. Michael's burns had been much worse than Daniel's. Both of them would be scarred for the rest of their lives. So would Emily.

She kept herself busy, so that the memories would have less chance of flooding her. At night, when she was all alone in her tiny room, and the only sounds were the ocean and her radio, she still thought about that night.

For now, it didn't matter. Only her parents and the police knew exactly where she was. She had not even told Morgan, hoping it would keep her safe. It had to be this way. As long as only a few people knew her location, it was less likely that someone would let it slip. It had been almost a year now, and she had no idea how long she would have to live her life like this. Michael might be gone, locked up indefinitely in the psychiatric ward back in Calgary, but he still sent postcards and gifts to her at her parents' home. In the letters, he pleaded with them to help him reunite with his fiancé.

And now Emily walked up the steep steps to her new home, a faint smile on her lips as she looked to her left to the harbour and the islands beyond. She turned back, about to open her door when she stopped suddenly, looking at the ornate mailbox fixed to the post of the high, narrow door-frame. Something she saw made her heart pound, her palms sweat. She didn't notice as her purse and carrying case slipped off her shoulder and fell to the stones.

Shortly after arriving here, her mail had been delivered to a post office box in the neighbouring village, just one more precaution to protect her location. Nothing addressed to her would reach this house.

But there it was. She shook as she reached for the small, blue envelope jutting out of the mail-box. Emily blinked, feeling the tears sting. She blinked again and looked. There was no envelope. The mailbox was empty.

It was always empty.

Chapter 23

I fix computers, I told them. It's what I do.

It was so easy to fool them. Almost too easy.

Smile when they speak to you, look into their eyes and respond appropriately to their ridiculous questions.

And now I am a trusted patient with high hopes of making a complete recovery. Best of all, they let me fix their computers. It was a great idea, really. They were sure it would help me in my recovery, make me feel useful and a part of society. Not to mention the money saved not using outside resources.

It was easy to track my Emily, once she and her parents began to e-mail each other regularly. Everyone thinks that wireless means untraceable. I know better. Everything leaves a trace, and sometimes it takes a little while to follow that path, but it's there. It's always there.

In her e-mails she never mentions me. That is good. That's the way we planned it. Throw them off, use misdirection, baffle them. You have to read between the lines, but there in the spaces she leaves blank are the words she sends to me.

In those blank spaces, I see what I mean to her and how much she needs to see me once more. And it will be soon. Even the doctors have begun to realize that I don't belong in a place like this. It was insulting, really. And Emily knew it as well.

I will be free soon and I will go to her so that we can be together again.